SWEET

First Edition

Published by The Nazca Plains Corporation
Las Vegas, Nevada
2011

ISBN: 978-1-61098-220-7
E-book: 978-1-61098-221-4

Published by

The Nazca Plains Corporation ®
4640 Paradise Rd, Suite 141
Las Vegas NV 89109-8000

PUBLISHER'S NOTE
Sweet is a work of fiction created wholly by Cameron Michaels' imagination. All characters are fictional and any resemblance to any persons living or deceased is purely by accident. No portion of this book reflects any real person or events.

Cover Photo, Arrow Studio
Art Director, Blake Stephens

SWEET

First Edition

Cameron Michaels

DEDICATION

I read this somewhere:

"There is no shame in not being loved, but in not loving."

To anyone and everyone who has been fortunate enough to find, experience, and embrace love.

ACKNOWLEDGEMENTS

With deepest gratitude and appreciation to Sam Weller and Jan Nguyen.

Special thanks to Jennifer Kirkland of World Web Content Writers. I had all the words—she made sense of them when they didn't. She punctuated, she added one or two and deleted a few, but most importantly, she cared about them as much as I did.

Last but by no means any less important, my family and friends. You supported all my efforts throughout this process. You are all so very important to me.

CONTENTS

CHAPTER 1

Turn Back and Wave

My mind was reeling. I was on overdrive. I couldn't shut it off and find a place of tranquility. In the darkness and silence of my condo, I sat alone. When the deafening silence and my raging thoughts became unbearable, I paced like a caged animal, arms crossed and locked, fighting hard to maintain control and to restrain the flood of emotion and tears. It didn't work most of the time. I felt reactionary impulses to scream, to break something, to slug the wall, and to put my fist through the door. I actually contemplated picking up one of the overstuffed leather chairs and catapulting it through the picture window.

These reactions were not in my nature, but I did feel them surfacing from within me. My skin prickled with anger and feelings of betrayal. I was slowly going crazy. I paced. I felt like a pressure cooker ready and waiting to explode. My mind continued to race. I was totally on edge. Something inside of me was going to snap—it was only a matter of time.

I had to calm down. What good was this doing? My behavior was so detrimental and unproductive. At the very least, I was wearing a path in the carpeting with all my pacing. *POSITIVE!* I fought against that thought. I had to change my discipline. I was wallowing in self-pity and anger. I calmed myself once, but then allowed those negative thoughts to return and I became consumed with them again.

I was processing everything that had happened in the past two days, trying to work through the emotional roller coaster. It was so easy to be angry and negative. Negativity was a way to maintain my defense mechanism, despite it tearing me apart. I had to feel those emotions; it was only natural to experience them, given the circumstances of what I had just endured. I also knew that it was destructive and harmful to dwell on them for any length of time.

"Think, Jeff. Think! Remember the delight, the joy, and the happiness of all that you experienced with him up until the past seventy-two hours." I kept thinking and pacing. I was trying to talk myself into changing my current thought process. I had done it once already; I know I could do it again. I had to. I kept thinking. *"Calm down. Breathe. Breathe deep, Jeff, and quit beating yourself up. There is nothing you can do about what has happened. It has happened and it is your reality now."*

"You have a choice, Jeff," the voice in my head kept reiterating. *"Be miserable and angry or calm yourself and remember the sweetness and moments shared."* I kept repeating that to myself, as my pacing slowed and I came to a stop in front of the living room window. I concentrated on the beauty of what he meant to me.

Did I hate him? NO! I loved him. I always will. This I know as fact. The ugliness of my mood slowly started to change. I felt the hateful thoughts and the hurt being exhumed from my mind and heart, as I started to talk myself into a more serene and peaceful place. The kinder and gentler thoughts started to prevail and began to replace the unfavorable. It was where I wanted to be mentally. I wanted to find resolution to what had happened.

I dried my face with my shirt sleeve and stared out the window into the darkness of night. There was no traffic, no one walking his dog, and the lake was motionless. The streets appeared empty. I found it a tad peculiar. There was no movement outside at all. It seemed that the world outside was void of life, similar to the way I was feeling inside. I stood in solitude, and thoughts of him standing behind me, holding me, infiltrated my mind. I didn't feel so alone.

Those were the thoughts I wanted to fill myself with—the thoughts of him and me together, carefree. My heart and soul began to warm; I actually began to smile. I managed to calm myself and found that I was depleted emotionally and I was physically spent. The mental processing of what had occurred was exhausting and took its toll on me. My body and mind ached for relief. There was no more anger. There were no more thoughts of betrayal.

There were only the slightest slivers of light from the streetlights below that illuminated the bedroom. I started removing my clothing. I was going to try to sleep or at least lie down and rest. It was time to bring this day to an end. The past three days were all merged together and situated me in an overload mode. I stood there undressing, blankly staring out the window. My own touch brought back thoughts of his touch and how it felt to be held.

Suddenly, there it was. It filled my nostrils—it was overpowering. It was his scent, that distinctive smell that was all his. My lungs ached as I struggled to inhale every molecule of the aroma, expanding my lungs beyond their capacity to capture it, never allowing his fragrance to escape in an exhale. It was part of me now and part of my DNA makeup. I never wanted to forget it or surrender it. It will be mine to retain selfishly and hold hostage forever.

Having finished undressing, I lay down on the bed and closed my eyes. Although I calmed myself enough to contemplate rest or even sleep, it eluded me. I couldn't shut my thought process off. Vivid images of him and our life together broke free of my mind's archives. A kaleidoscope of memories cascaded upon me and danced pleasantly before me. A single tear trickled from my right eye, as I revisited everything from the beginning to this exact moment. It was a tear of joy and one of happiness, as there is nothing as sacred as a love share

SUMMER. The Beginning.

It was a cool day for mid-July in Chicago. The wind was gusty at times. The sky was clear, but there was a little bite in the air. I had taken the day off from work—a mental health day, as I called them. I needed to be by the water. The lake was beautiful that day. The sun danced on the ripples. The beautiful sparkles reflecting off the small waves were blinding. I had ridden my bike along the lake for about an hour when I decided to stop and take in the beauty of the lake and the day. I stood there gazing out over the vast body of water, reflective in thought. My life, what it was, where it is, and what it might become—all the things a man my age thinks about in his solitude. The wind was caressing my cheek and mussing up my hair. An easy calm came over me as I watched the small waves meander back and forth.

The water is my comfort and serenity. Whenever I feel lost or a bit out of control, I head to the lake for the calming effects it has on me. Being by the water is a soothing, calming, and cleansing experience. No matter how whacked out the world around me seems, it all becomes sorted out and back in place when I am by the water.

I had been alone for seven years. I isolated myself from the social world, by choice. It was time for me to rebuild a life. I knew this in my heart. I had many questions. Had I waited too long to begin again? Had opportunities passed me by? What was I searching for? All questions that I had no answers for, even by the lake.

I enjoyed my life. It was quiet and well structured, and I was at peace with the niche that I had carved out. Perhaps it was just that—being comfortable—that was the problem.

I struggled with the thought of a committed relationship. We all want someone to love and to love us, and I was no exception. I lived alone, but I was not lonely. I had a phenomenal circle of close friends and a family bond that was very sacred to me. There were times that I craved companionship and commitment, and felt envious of my friends, straight or gay, that had that. Then at other times I wasn't so sure. I saw all the drama, the emotional highs and lows, and the struggles that they all endured. I wasn't so sure that I wanted to put myself through that.

I won't be in a relationship just to be in one or for the bragging rights of having one. Yet there was this nagging feeling at times that something was missing. I was conflicted. On one hand, I was very happy with the way my life was and how it had evolved. Then there were those times that I knew I needed to make a change. I wanted to share my life with someone. At times I actually thought I needed that—not to complete it, but to add balance and symmetry to it. Maybe I was struggling with knowing that I might have to give up things, make compromises, and lose myself in the relationship. I just couldn't figure it out. It might just be that the right guy hadn't crossed my path yet.

How it manifests itself in your life or what you call it is unimportant. What is important is that we all have this guardian, and it is this guardian that guides us through life. I am firm in my conviction that we all have a life map and it is that higher power that wrote it for us. So, sometimes it is not our time frame that dictates life events—it is the time frame that has been written for us. We just have to trust in that higher power and our own convictions.

Having spent an extended amount of time contemplating the questions that haunted me, I decided to start back for the remainder of my bike ride. Out of my right peripheral vision, I noticed another biker coming in my direction. I was in the middle of my push off from the wall when I noticed him. Having already started my push, I couldn't easily come to a stop, but managed to before colliding with him. My front tire dug into the dirt and the rear end of my bike came off the ground and swung to the left. I was struggling to maintain my balance. He veered off around me and came to a stop.

The biker stood straddling the frame of his bike, turned, and looked at me. I couldn't assess his demeanor right away. I was feeling a bit awkward, having almost caused a collision.

"I'm sorry. I didn't mean to cut you off," I offered.

"You didn't—just didn't want us to crash. That was a close call. My name is Pete," he replied, extending his hand.

"Hi, Peter," I answered. Taking his hand in mine, I received a good solid grip and sturdy shake. "I am Jeffrey."

He looked me straight in the eyes, never glancing left or right. He smirked after our introductions. I became a bit irritated. I was unsure why someone I had just met would think that I or my name was a source of humor. I looked at him, a bit puzzled. I wasn't sure what to make of the expression or smirk. Although I had just met him, it was hard for me to think that this splendid-looking man could be so crude. Perhaps it was that he was just a bit nervous, having almost collided with me, albeit accidentally and my fault. I stood there evaluating him, taking in every detail. Something about him instantly intrigued me.

He was about six foot four, I estimated. His hair was thick and dark brown, and it shined and shimmered in the sunlight. His complexion was smooth and bronzed by the summer tanning season, although I suspected he had a dark complexion by nature. He had big brown eyes that melted my very soul. He was in fit condition, with a nicely shaped chest that the tightness of his T-shirt revealed as he stretched forward to shake hands. His stomach looked flat—not a six-pack flat, just trim. He had solid legs covered with dark hair. He was no stranger to a healthy lifestyle. He wasn't overly worked out; he had a natural build, complemented by physical work, I assumed.

I noticed his hands. They were groomed, soft, and, most importantly, wore no wedding ring. His voice was soft and deep, and he spoke directly to me. He had deliberate eye contact—not the scary ax murderer stares, but one that told you that you had his undivided attention. He had full lips that turned up into a smile that also melted my soul. I stood there evaluating my new acquaintance, thinking that I could definitely spend time with him.

Snapping myself out of my concentration and evaluation of him, I spoke, a bit put off by the snickers my name had elicited.

"Is there something you find humorous about my name?" I asked.

"No, Jeff," he said with a soft laugh. "I am sorry if I gave you that impression. Our introduction just reminded me of some of the funny things that I saw in a play last night. Maybe you have heard about it. It was a two-act play with just one actor and audience participation. It was about a Catholic school, and the nun took you through…"

I excitedly interrupted almost immediately. "Yeah, yeah, yeah! *Late Night Catechism.* I saw that a couple of months ago at the Royal George Theater. She goes through the audience and picks out people to torment."

"Yep! She nabbed me! It was awful," he replied, laughing.

"Me, too! I was in the crosshairs," I replied with a laugh. "I went with a couple of friends from work and we couldn't have been in worse seats. Ground Zero, I think."

We stood there and laughed about what we'd each suffered during the performance. We took turns talking about the realism of the play and the simplicity of the set; how we got caught up and really believed that we were in that classroom. We also discussed how it brought back memories of our childhood schooling. We both wanted to see it again.

"So, you see, I wasn't making fun of your name," he said reassuringly. "It is just that the nuns always use the full name. When I introduced myself as Pete, you replied with 'Peter' and used your full name. It was what the nuns always did and what she did in the play that night. It just struck me funny. I am sorry if I offended you." He smiled. I melted.

"Sorry if I was a bit irritated when I thought you were making fun of my name," I said. "After all, it is my name and I am a bit partial to it." I smiled and stared him in the eyes.

"Totally understandable," he answered. "So, is it Jeffrey or Jeff?"

"Jeffrey is what I prefer, but I will answer to almost anything… within reason, that is," I said with a chuckle.

"So, Jeff…rey, what brings you to the lakefront today? Just out for a ride, enjoying a day when it's not as crowded as on the weekends?" he asked.

I explained my mental health day from work, how I was always down by the water and how I try to ride my bike as much as I can while the weather permits. I found myself falling into an easy rhythm of conversation with my new acquaintance. It was hard for me not to stare at him. He created a stir in me that I had not felt in a long time. It was a bit unnerving, and yet exciting. I continued to look out over the water as we talked. I would occasionally look over at him, only to find his gaze was fixed on me.

I was not uncomfortable with his gaze, as I was forcing myself not to stare at him. I was very attracted to him, at least physically at this point. *"This is crazy,"* I thought, *"being attracted to him so quickly."* Then I would think, *"Go with the flow of things and allow yourself to enjoy this moment."* I was getting a bit nervous; I was so inept with initial meetings.

I would start to ask questions or make comments, then immediately withdraw. I was getting all anxious inside. It happened all the time when I was in a one-on-one situation like this. Small talk has never been one of my strongest suits. He was holding up most of the conversation. I did interject some questions and comments, but he appeared to be more comfortable. I was, however, becoming more at ease as the conversation continued.

The conversation moved along comfortably, seeming to be never ending—there was never a lapse or gap. I was very shocked at how easy it was for me to talk with him. I am very reserved at first—painfully shy—but this man had a fix on me that I could not explain. It was as if we had known each other for years—decades even.

As we talked, I learned where he lived and what he did for a living, and that he owned his own business. I learned about his family, their names, and where they lived. He had a connection to his family that was admirable. He was loyal to his friends and most importantly to himself. I liked that about him. He was not pretentious in his delivery of his life facts—in fact, they came across as very modest.

He broke the conversation. "Hey, I am thirsty. Know where we might get a drink of water or some bottled water?"

"We?" I thought. *"He is assuming we are riding together now, or maybe he is hinting that he wants to. Is he showing interest in me?"* I am so bad about this type of thing. I never know when someone is interested in me. I don't usually have men of his caliber paying attention to me, or so I think. I have been told differently by friends. My friends say that I just don't get it. Perhaps they are right. My reaction—or lack of it—comes across as me being uninterested or even snobbish. Snobbishness is not one of the traits that I possess.

"Sure, there is a public water fountain just around the bend, but there is a small place on the beach, just up the bike path, for bottled water," I explained. "I am headed that way for the rest of my ride before turning around and heading back towards home. It is just up this way." I pointed in the general direction.

With that, I put my foot on the pedal and started off, hoping that he might follow. I also knew that I would have stopped in a short distance and found the courage to invite him to join me. I didn't have to, however—I heard him call out from behind me: "Hey Jeff…rey, mind if I tag along?"

My heart raced as I looked back and nonchalantly replied, "Yeah, sure. Come on. I will show you where you can get that drink of water."

Looking back at Peter, I saw him smiling one of those easy, comfortable smiles I would come to know and enjoy. He caught up with me, and we rode together down the path to the public fountain. The conversation continued as we spoke of places we had traveled, our favorite meals, and our least favorite televisions shows. Conversation flowed easily from one subject to another, but somehow all the topics tied in together.

After a short stop at the fountain, I was getting ready to push off again, when a puzzled look appeared on Peter's face. I dismissed it, figuring that I must have said something a bit confusing or possibly out of line. I have a habit of doing that so often, especially when I am nervous or anxious.

I think something is hilarious in my head and when it pops out the mouth, it doesn't always have the same effect. Just before I started to roll away, Peter began to ask the question that triggered his expression.

"Jeffrey…ummm…I don't want to offend you, but I want to ask you something. Ah, never mind," he stammered.

"What is it? I am not easily offended. OK, maybe when I think someone is making fun of my name," I said in jest and laughed. "Ask me whatever you would like."

"Well…ummm. Are you gay?" he finally asked.

Now, to me that was a very silly question. I have been gay all my life, so I figure it is just obvious to everyone. I am not flamboyant in my actions or mannerisms and have been told by friends that it is hard to tell which "team" I play for, as they put it.

"You don't act gay," they say. "You carry yourself differently than most gay men." They are stereotyping, but I guess it is true. I don't put it out there. I would never deny who I was, if asked, but I don't volunteer the information, either. It is a private thing with me. It is part of my life, not my whole life.

I simply turned and looked directly into those beautiful big brown eyes and smiled. "Yep."

I pushed off and started riding again. Soon we were leisurely riding side by side. The conversation continued as he asked questions about my job, where I lived, and what I did in my spare time. We discussed living in the city versus the 'burbs. We touched on current events in the city and in the world. He asked direct questions, precise and unobtrusive.

The conversation bounced back and forth between his life and mine. I learned more about him, and he discovered more about me. I amazed myself at how free I was with my information. I usually am a little more guarded. It just seemed right to share the things that I did.

When we reached Navy Pier, we both seemed to know instinctively that we had reached our turning point. We could have continued on around the bend, south to the Yacht Club, but we didn't. At the same time, we turned our bikes around and rode back in the direction we had just come from.

On the way back, I found out more about his life. He lived north of the city. He was one of three children from an Italian family. He was the middle child, as I was, and he had a great bond with his family. He loved his parents and his two sisters deeply. The bond between them was extremely strong. When he spoke of his business and his employees, he spoke of it as if it were a family. He sounded very committed to them.

His office was in a three-story walk-up building. The office occupied the lower floor, and his residence was the upper two floors, which he had converted into a loft-style living space. I shared some details about my condo and how surprised I was that I had found such a wonderful place to live. I told him I lived in East Lakeview and didn't get specific as to the address.

We exchanged ideas on decorating our places, both agreeing that it is never done, discussing what we wanted to do with our space and what we wouldn't or didn't want to do. Keep it simple seemed to be the underlying tone.

When he spoke of his life, it was as a blessing rather than bragging. He was completely unpretentious. There was a pride in the accomplishments, along with an appreciation that they could all be gone tomorrow. He didn't take anything for granted.

The whole time we rode, I was thinking, *"This guy is not for real. There has to be something wrong with him. But what?"* I had not yet discovered that.

We were coming up to my turnoff point, a tunnel under Lake Shore Drive that takes you off the park side of the drive and puts you on the residential side. It was also here that he had parked his car in one of the park's parking lots.

"Well, Peter, this is my stopping point," I said. "I need to head into the tunnel and get home."

"So, where is it that you actually live? Can you see it from here?" he asked.

I pointed up to the mid-rise building across the drive and said, "Right there."

"Right there?" he asked with disbelief.

"Yeah, right there, on the fourteenth floor. This is my view," I said, pointing at the tennis courts, baseball diamonds, and the harbor.

"Well, you said you lived in this neighborhood, but you didn't say you lived right on the drive! I am impressed. What a wonderful place to live," he said.

"No one is more impressed than I am," I answered. "I still don't believe that I live here, either. I fell into a great deal and couldn't pass it up. It is a great space—nice views and everything is within walking distance."

"I bet the view is nice from up there," he said.

"It is, especially from the twenty-ninth floor—the rooftop deck," I responded.

"I am sure it is a great view of the city and lake. I would love to…" His statement trailed off.

All of a sudden, I was all anxious and nervous again. I wasn't sure what he was going to say. I couldn't read his face or body language, given the fact that I hadn't known him that long. I quickly contemplated my options. It was in the brain and out the mouth before I knew what I was saying.

"It is a wonderful view. Would you like to come up and see it?" I asked.

"Yes, I think I would," he replied.

With that, we headed through the tunnel, under Lake Shore Drive, and up on my side of the street. We crossed the street and entered the building. I took a minute to say hello to my favorite doorman, and we exchanged some pleasantries. Peter and I rode up in the service elevator. I took another full assessment of my new friend. I was smiling the whole trip up to the fourteenth floor.

"You have a wonderful smile," he said as he followed me out the elevator and to the door of the condo.

"Thanks," I said, feeling a bit giddy and foolish. "Here we are— home. Well, my home," I said. *"Damn it, Jeff, don't let your nervousness get to you! Don't do anything stupid. He is here, he must be interested, you are interested in him, and you had a wonderful bike ride together. Don't blow it!"* ran through my mind. I opened the door and suggested where he should park his bike. He stood and looked around, not moving.

"Great place, Jeff," he said.

"Look around, make yourself comfortable. Excuse the mess," I said, walking him around, showing him my home.

"Looks good to me," he commented. "I don't see any mess."

"Can I get you something to drink? Water, coffee, or maybe there is a beer in there?" I offered.

"No, thanks on the beer. I have a commitment later this evening. Water will be fine," he replied.

"Make yourself at home," I said, pointing at the living room. "I'll get the water and we can go up to the deck."

"It is easy to make yourself comfortable. Your home is very nice, and you have it arranged well. I wish I could do this to my place," he said.

"Thanks. I change it around now and then, but I like the way it is right now. I may keep it this way," I responded.

I moved from the kitchen to the living room and handed Peter his water. He smiled and thanked me. We moved to the windows to check out the view from there. As he stood looking out at the harbor and lake, a smile came to his face. His eyes danced like those of a child on Christmas morning. He was watching the sailboats gliding over the water. He appeared relaxed as he moved from the window to one of the overstuffed chairs.

"I could sit here for hours just looking out at the view," he said as he sat down.

"It is nice, and I do. I especially love it in the morning when the sailboats are leaving the harbor and the sun is just coming up. It is so serene and peaceful," I said.

"Morning coffee and this view. What a way to start the day," he remarked.

My mind was saying, *"And you to share it with..."* I wanted to sit there for a while and just look at him. He was such a handsome man. His mannerisms were soft and quiet. He appeared to be so content with who he was and what his life was. I hated to end this moment, but after all, we did come up to see the view from the deck.

In the elevator we went, up to the twenty-eighth floor. We had to go up a flight of steps to the deck. It had warmed up a little and the sky was clear. I had noticed that while we were riding, some billowing clouds were skimming across the sky above us. There were no traces of them now, just a steady breeze. The wind was so blustery at times, it'd push you back a step.

We went to the railing and looked over the lake and then to the south side for the view of the city. We walked around to the north, the direction he lived. We were like tourists, pointing out different sights. He pointed north and went through this elaborate oration about a certain building and said that he could see his place from here. I was pretty excited about that, and then he told me he was just joking. I fell for it, and he laughed at me. I laughed at myself for being so smitten with him that I actually believed what he was saying.

He apologized for making fun of me and explained how far north he actually lived, saying that he would show me sometime. I let it pass, thinking that it was just first-time meeting nicety.

I am not a big baseball fan, but most of my friends and new acquaintances enjoy the view of Wrigley Field. We moved to the west railing and took in the view of the stadium, which takes up a full city block. It is pretty cool to have one of the granddads of baseball fields basically in my backyard. It's kind of fun to have the bragging rights of living so close to Wrigley.

Looking again to the south, our eyes were drawn to the majestic skyscrapers of the city—the Sears Tower and the Hancock Building being the most notable. It is as if they are the guardians of the city and not just landmarks. As we scanned the horizon, we saw all the neighborhoods and suburbs that stretched farther than our eyes could detect. Each neighborhood and suburb was unique in its makeup. Billowing smokestacks, church steeples, and an assortment of residential and corporate buildings comprised most of the metro area.

There was movement everywhere we looked. The streets were busy with cars and bikes. The "L" wound its way through the city. If we looked to the northwest, just above the horizon, we could actually see planes arriving and departing from O'Hare. We were in agreement that this had to be the best city to live in.

We moved back to the east banister of the deck again and looked over the lake. The blues were brilliant, and the sun only magnified their beauty. There was a slight chop to the water now, which I attributed to the winds. Lake Michigan is the third largest of the five Great Lakes, and the fifth-largest lake in the world. The lake stretches 307 miles from north to south and spreads 118 miles east to west. It is the only one that is entirely in the United States, and not shared with Canada. The lake isn't just a source of beauty—it is also a source of recreation and commerce.

The flight pattern of O'Hare must have changed. Arriving aircraft were banking around over the lake, getting into their landing patterns. Aircraft of all sizes were lining up. Peter and I watched as some of the international arrivals flew by, and I named off the ones I could, using their unique paint jobs and trademark tails as identifiers. We made a game of it.

After what seemed like only a few seconds, but actually was about thirty minutes, he said that he had to be getting home.

"Yeah, that commitment you mentioned," I said.

"Yep, very important date," he explained. "I promised that I wouldn't cancel again."

"Date! Damn it! He is seeing someone else!" my mind screamed. I managed to say, "Well, you don't want to be late. That is a bad first impression."

"No first impression needed. We've know each other for a few years," he said.

"That is even more reason not to be late," I said, while thinking, *"Great. It is a long-term dating thing."*

I was trying to remain calm and together. My face always seems to give me away. I am not sure whether he picked up on that or not. My nonverbal behavior says much more than I would like it to. I don't have a poker face at all. He just chuckled and smiled at me again as we walked down the stairs to the elevators.

"I am actually looking forward to this date," he continued. "Can't say that I want to see *Finding Nemo*, but a promise to a nine-year-old is a promise. Because of work I had to cancel last weekend, so I'd better not tonight."

I laughed out loud, more at myself than at this statement. A ton of questions flooded my head, questions that I could not ask at the moment and that were none of my business. If he wanted to share that with me, he would. Did he have an ex-wife? Was it his child? I was beginning to think I might be finding out what was wrong with this man. It would be his past. At this point, it was nothing that I would have to concern myself with. After all, we had just known each other for a couple of hours. But an ex-wife and a kid, if that was what it was—I wasn't so sure I wanted to be involved in that kind of arrangement.

"Be serious, Jeff! Relax and just go with the flow of things for now!" I shouted to myself.

We reached my condo and went inside. We talked for a short time before he said he had to leave. He asked to use the restroom before the drive home. I pointed him in the direction he needed to be and went into the living room. As I stood there thinking about my acquaintance, I kept returning to my thought: *"What a guy!"* I was thinking things I hadn't thought in a long time. I was feeling something I couldn't place my finger on. It was slightly disturbing and uncomfortable, yet exhilarating. Knowing me, I would analyze it and try to figure out what it was about him that captivated me so. I needed to trust my intuition. It had never failed me in the past.

What was it? He was handsome, had a great sense of humor, was interesting to talk with, and had one hell of a killer smile. There was more, though—much more. There was something about him that was so familiar and extremely appealing to me. It wasn't just physical, although that in itself was nothing to scoff at. It was some type of spiritual connection. I could be wrong, though I hoped not. Our meeting was more than just a chance encounter.

I heard the bathroom door open, and I quickly snapped back from my wandering thoughts.

"I'm sorry, Jeffrey. I really need to go. Thanks for the bike ride, the hospitality, and the great view. I enjoyed it," he said.

He seemed a bit anxious now, unsure what to do next. I could relate—I was feeling the same way. He fussed with his bike a little and arranged it so that he could easily walk it out the door. He took a couple of steps and stopped, then fixed his eyes to mine. It was as if I were in some type of hypnotic hold. I looked into those deep, dark eyes. I could see there was something he wanted to say. He seemed unsure of what it was or how he might say it.

"What is it, Peter? Did you misplace something? You look a bit perplexed," I said carefully.

"I am not very good with this, Jeffrey. I always mess up things like this. I usually make a total fool of myself," he said quietly.

That was hard for me to believe. I couldn't imagine that he would have difficulty with anything. He made talking and being around him so comfortable, in the short time we had spent together. What could he be unsure of? Was this where I was going to find out what was wrong with him?

"You don't impress me as the type of guy that would be unsure of himself. I get the feeling that you are pretty easygoing and self-assured," I said.

"Usually I am, until it comes to things like this," he replied.

"Things like what?" I asked.

"All right. Here goes." He cleared his throat and shifted back and forth a little.

He was looking so boyishly innocent, so unsure of himself, not knowing what he wanted to say or ask—almost unsure of whether he should trust his words and voice. He looked up again and met my stare. I could see he was trying to find either the confidence or the right words. He took a deep breath and let out a low, barely audible sigh.

"So, would you like to have coffee or dinner with me sometime?" It just came blurting out.

"How about both?" I replied without hesitation.

All the nervousness and anxiety exited his body. I could almost see it dissipate from him. His shoulders relaxed and he smiled. I melted.

"SWEET! Great. That is just great," he said with a huge grin.

"Thanks for asking," I quipped. "I am glad you asked, because I was trying to muster the nerve and wasn't sure how or when I was going to ask you the same thing. I have a terrible time with that stuff, too."

"I wasn't sure I could. I get so nervous about that stuff. We hardly know each other, and I doubted that I would run into you again. I had to say or do something. Silly, huh, for a grown man?" He laughed.

He stepped around his bike and extended his hand again. I took his hand and shook it. After the handshake should have ended, we were still standing there holding hands. I was amused and smiled. I didn't want to laugh, but it was funny to me. I looked down at our hands and back up to his face. It was as if we both realized at the same time we were standing in my living room holding hands. We both chuckled a nervous laugh. He released his grip and moved towards the door.

"All right, then, I will call you and we can see how our schedules look and set it up," he said.

"I'm not so sure that can happen, Peter," I responded.

"Huh?" A puzzled look crossed his face.

"Can't call if you don't have my phone number," I explained with a laugh.

"Oh, yeah! Pretty silly of me! I told you I am not good at this sort of thing," he said.

"Me, either," I agreed.

I searched my desk for one of my personal business cards, which had my phone number and e-mail address on it. I had them made after I moved to Chicago and into the condo. They were useful to hand out when a pen and paper were not available. My best friend Michael called them trick cards. He gave me way too much credit.

I decided to ride down in the elevator with him and walk him to his car. There was no conversation, just glances and smiles. He appeared pleased, and I knew I was. We reached the first floor, and out to the street we went. It wasn't until we reached the other side of Lake Shore Drive that he spoke.

"I am so glad I got to meet you today," he stopped and said.

"Me, too. It has been a pleasure. I have enjoyed it," I replied with a smile.

"I will call you. Promise. I am not like other guys who say they will and don't," he said reassuringly.

"I'll be looking forward to that. I've gotten the impression that you are not like most other guys," I said.

"Really? I didn't think I made that much of a first impression," he said with a smirk.

"I was thinking I didn't do so hot in that area," I said.

"Not at all! The moment I saw you standing there, straddling your bike, something inside me took over and I wanted to meet you. I am bad with cold introductions like that, but I forced myself to do it," he explained, continuing, "You had passed me and I turned to see where you were going. I didn't know what I was going to do or say, but I just felt like I had to somehow meet you."

"Glad you did," I said.

"My car is right here." He stopped and put the bike on the trunk rack. "Thanks for walking me down."

"Didn't want you to get lost. If you did, then I would lose out on that dinner and coffee. So, it was a bit selfish of me," I joked.

"Thanks again, and I will call you later," he said.

"Drive safe. After all, there is a nine-year-old counting on you and Nemo tonight!" I joked.

With that said, I turned and walked away. I didn't want one of those awkward what to do next moments. Do I kiss him or shake hands again? I guess I could have slapped him on the back and shoulders and trotted off. No, a simple turn and walk away, then pause and turn back and wave. Yeah, that was it. That is what I did. When I turned, he was standing there, leaning back against his vehicle watching me walk away. We exchanged smiles and waved, and through the tunnel I went.

CHAPTER 2

The One? Plus Six and Two

As I walked back through the tunnel, I was smiling so hard that my cheeks hurt, and I knew that I was going to have perma-grin for the remainder of the afternoon and evening. I was feeling things that I had not experienced in a while. I was walking on air.

"WHAT AN AMAZING MAN!" my brain screamed. I floated through the tunnel back to my building. I crossed the road and was up in my house before I knew it. It was like being on autopilot. My mind played back the whole afternoon. I remembered things that he said. How he talked and used his hands. His expressions came to mind, as I reviewed the conversations we had. I was smiling still. I was also going to be late for dinner with friends if I didn't get moving. A quick run through the shower, costume change, and off I went.

My friends quizzed me on my mood and made some speculation as to my—as they put it—nauseatingly good mood. Their comments were all in jest, and my silence only fueled their playful comments. We had a good time.

I wasn't ready to tell anyone about meeting Peter. I wanted to keep it my own little secret for now. They would have called me silly, among other things, if I tried to explain what I was feeling. They would have been correct. How could I possibly know what kind of guy he is, in the short time I spent with him? Sometimes you just know. It is called instinct, gut feelings, or that certain intangible something none of us can ever quite put his finger on. But we feel it.

After returning from dinner later that night, about 10:00, I decided to check my e-mail and do a little of the work I brought home the day before, or maybe surf a little before going to bed. To my surprise and excitement, there was an offline message waiting for me.

Jeff,

I had a great time this afternoon. Thanks. Was great to meet you and I look forward to our dinner and coffee.

Pete(r)

As I read it again, I realized that my face was hurting from smiling so hard again. I felt a sense of joy that I had not felt in a long time. *"I am being foolish,"* my inner voice of doubt argued. It was just a chance meeting. Or was it? He was incredible, handsome, and, for the short time that I had known him, polite and sincere. I was looking forward to the coffee and dinner date.

I looked at the monitor. Several questions crossed my mind. What should I do? Should I reply? What do I say? I was being a foolish high school teenager, I decided. I kind of liked the feeling that gave me. It was a phenomenal feeling that I had not experienced much in the past few years.

I reached for the keyboard to return the message. I couldn't believe how conflicted I was about what to say back. I am pretty direct and forward with my feelings and thoughts. *"Why do I want to be so careful with this? Why does it feel so important?"*

I hate this sort of thing—the early dating stuff. I kept telling myself to just write something, anything! I looked skyward for guidance, as if God were going to jump in. *"Stop being silly and just jot something down and send it!"*

I placed my fingers on the keys and then removed them. I repeated this movement two or three times. I finally took a deep breath and started typing. It just flowed out, and I didn't think too much about what I was typing.

Peter,

I also enjoyed the afternoon and meeting you. I am looking forward to our dinner / coffee as well. Thanks for sharing the view from the roof deck.

Jeffrey

I sent the message via the cyber highway and decided to shut the computer down and not do the work or surfing I originally thought I might. There was a chime alert and another message:

You are home and up. How was your evening? Nemo was rescued and all is good in the world. Can I call you?

I replied:

Thank goodness Nemo is safe. Sure.

It seemed as though I had just hit the send button when the phone rang. Did he predial it? Was he just waiting for a response to his instant message? I really didn't care—he was calling.

"Hello there, mister." His voice was smooth as velvet.

"Hey, how was your evening? Little one in bed?" I asked.

"Doing well. I survived a dinner of mac and cheese, hot dogs, and Doritos. Actually, she is back with my sister Dianna. What did you do this evening?" he asked.

"Ah, so it is Uncle Peter. I had dinner with friends and we went to our favorite Mexican restaurant and then to coffee," I said.

"What night are you free for our dinner?" he asked.

"Any night should be good. I don't think my social calendar is overflowing," I replied in a playful tone.

"Great. How about next Tuesday?" he asked.

"I think that should work. No, wait… I have a meeting that night I have to attend," I said.

"OK, then. Let's try Wednesday night," he suggested.

"That is good with me. I work until 5:00, and with the train ride I should be home around 6:30," I said.

"Where would you like to go? I have a couple of ideas, but wasn't sure where you would like to go," he said.

We talked about different restaurants and settled on one that neither one of us had been to. I kept thinking the whole time, *"This guy is great, unbelievable. He seems so sincere and genuine. He doesn't appear to be self-absorbed. There has to be something the matter with him—there just has to be!"*

My luck with meeting men that summer had not been all that great. There had been a string of married men, men who didn't know what they were looking for and were having major midlife crises. Most of the men were looking for someone younger and/or a one-night stand or friends with benefits sort of thing. I wasn't interested in any of that or them. I thought it was difficult dating when I was younger, but it was even more difficult now, I was finding out.

The conversation took several turns here and there on different subjects. We talked about local events, national events, and some of the silly entertainment news. We ventured into religion and spirituality, but I stayed away from politics. The afterlife conversation was extremely interesting, and we found ourselves on the same page, for the most part.

The topics just seemed to flow from one subject to another. To talk to him was effortless now. My initial anxiety seemed to have vanished. I didn't have any concerns of being considered stupid for my ideas or thoughts. I found that I could talk about anything with him. Neither one of us realized what time it was, until the first yawn was detected.

"Sorry, didn't mean to yawn in your ear," he said quickly.

"I think we both did it at the same time," I replied.

"Maybe so. I'm not sure if I am ready to hang up or want to," he said.

"Nice of you to say, Peter, but I have an early day tomorrow and so do you," I responded.

"I will call you tomorrow sometime. Have a great night," he said.

"Good night. You have a good evening, too," I said.

I turned the phone off, lay back on the bed, and smiled. I replayed the conversation in my head again. I felt so uplifted and happy. Yep, happy was what I was feeling.

I hate the dating stuff—it was starting to happen to me. There's that queasy feeling in your stomach—a good feeling, but a little uncomfortable in some ways. There is all the other stuff that goes along with the beginning stages of dating. There are the insecurities we feel about ourselves. There are those feelings of having to always put our best foot forward. What is the right thing to say and what to wear? These are just a few of the things.

There are other questions as well. Does he find me appealing? Can I keep his interest in a conversation? What will happen when he really gets to know me? How often should I e-mail him or call him? Things like that always seem to clog my head when I start dating someone. I am not alone. As much as we don't want to admit it, we all suffer from dating anxiety.

All these thoughts and then some were running through my head. It was like the ticker tape at the stock exchange and I couldn't turn it off. I kept telling myself that it was way too soon to be thinking those things and to breathe. It wasn't working.

I stripped off my clothes, flinging them into the clothes hamper and dry cleaning bag. I went through the house and turned off the lights, making sure everything was in its place for my early rise in the morning. I had just rolled onto the bed when the phone rang. I wasn't pleased. It was late and I needed to be up early, and it also interrupted my thoughts of Peter.

I answered the phone in a not so pleasant tone: "Hello?"

"Jeffrey, it's Pete," he said.

My voice softened. "Hey. What's up?"

"I just wanted to say good night again," he replied.

"How nice of you," I responded.

"Did I interrupt anything or catch you in the middle of something?" he asked.

"No, I just got undressed and was lying here thinking of you," I answered.

SHIT! What did I say that for? I sounded like a perv or something. DAMN IT. Well, I can't take it back now.

"Hmmm, naked and thinking of me. I like the sound of that. Of course, I am assuming you are naked?" he said in jest.

"As a matter of fact, I am," I replied.

"SWEET! Nice to have someone thinking about you while they are that way. Hey, give me a minute to turn off a couple of lights and I will join you on this end," he said.

I heard the phone being set down and a bunch of background noise. He came back to the phone once and checked to make sure I was still there. I confirmed that I wasn't going anywhere at the moment and he set the phone down again. There was a light breeze coming through the windows. It was a nice evening out and a great temperature for sleeping.

"You there?" he asked.

"Yep, I was just waiting for you to return," I responded.

"I had to check the doors, turn off the lights, and get out of my clothes, so I could join you here," he explained.

"This isn't going to be one of those kinds of phone calls, is it?" I asked with a smirk.

"What kind of call would that be?" he asked with mock innocence.

I recognized a playful tone in his voice. He assured me that his intentions were totally honorable. The conversation picked up where we left off the first time. The subjects and topics were mainly silly and lighthearted. We talked about our mutual appreciation for sleeping naked. Although we both owned a pair or two, we shared a mutual dislike for boxer underwear. We talked about thirty minutes and said good night again.

I lay back and closed my eyes. The thoughts drifted lightly through my head, like light, fluffy clouds on a beautiful spring day. I was feeling so comfortable and content. I snickered at myself, thinking about what a hopeless romantic I truly was. He touched that soft spot in me. I didn't think it was a put-on. I felt it was genuine.

I got the impression that Peter might be a romantic, too. I liked that thought. The last thoughts I had before drifting off to sleep that night were of him. How sweet of him for calling back. Smiling, I rolled over, grabbed a pillow, curled up, and slept.

Anxiety, scattered brained and giddy....

When I woke the next morning, my first thoughts were of him. As I went through my morning routine, I was smiling again, still. What a wonderful day I had the day before. I was enjoying the rebirth of those lost or hidden feelings—those feelings I thought were long ago abandoned.

After my shower, I poured a cup of coffee and sat at the computer. I read the news and my e-mail. All was right in my world that morning. I thought back to the conversations we had on the phone and smiled. I was feeling giddy. Yep. That was it—GIDDY. It suited me. I liked the feel of it.

I went through my workday easily. Things were good all day, and I am sure it had everything to do with what had transpired the day before. I thought about calling him and discarded the idea immediately. He said that he would call me, and I made myself a promise that morning that I wasn't going to call him. I wasn't going to get all anxious about this new interest. I wanted it to play out like it was going to and not force anything. I picked up the phone and started to dial... I hung the phone up. I was being silly.

I finished up at work and made my way to the train for the commute home. It was an uneventful ride on the first train, and I was a bit anxious to get home. My cell rang as I took my seat on the second train of my commute.

I totally forgot that had I agreed to meet my best friend Michael for dinner, but I assured him that I would be there. I met him at the restaurant, and we talked about the events that had happened since we last saw each other. I didn't tell him about Peter. I wasn't really sure why, but I didn't.

Michael was insistent about the fact that, as he saw it, I needed to get out more and meet someone. He was worried that I didn't have anyone "special" in my life. I listened politely and agreed. It would be great to meet the dream guy, I told him. I kept the fact that I thought I might have met him a secret—for the time being, anyway. I don't know why I needed to remain so private about meeting Peter. Maybe it was because I thought I would jinx it if I spoke about it. Maybe it was too early; after all, I had only met him the day before. I would tell him all about it eventually; when I knew that there was something to tell.

With dinner finished, I made my way home. It was a good day, but a long one. I noticed a spring in my step as I walked home. I was feeling great.

I got home later than I normally do, especially after getting up so early that morning. I reached my building and entered. I was greeted by Robert, my favorite doorman. It was always a pleasure to stop and talk with him. He never had a bad word about anyone or anything. He did, however, have the latest scoop about the scandals, hot topics, and events that surrounded the building. It was never conveyed in a malicious gossipy manner, but as a source of amusement and entertainment. I inquired about Mrs. Robert, as I called her, and was told that she was getting the itch to travel to Las Vegas. This seemed to have Robert a bit concerned, but he laughed as he told me he conceded and agreed to take her, adding that conceding was only a stall tactic.

Once inside with the door locked, I started my usual routine of stripping off the day's clothing and getting comfortable. I hated being in clothing all day, and I so enjoyed the freedom of walking around my condo naked. I thought of Peter and checked my computer for an e-mail from him. None, DAMN IT! Checking the phone next, I saw the message light blinking at me. I listened to the four messages and made some notes. None of the calls were from him, and I would make the return calls later or tomorrow.

Fussing with this and that, I finished a small project that I had started a couple of days prior. It was late and I readied myself for bed. It had been a long day. I lay down and got comfortable, settling in for a very welcome night of sleep. I started drifting off. I was in that trance-like state between awake and asleep when I was jolted into reality with the ringing of the phone. I stumbled across the room and answered it.

"Jeffrey, did I wake you?" Peter asked. My skin tingled as he spoke to me.

"No. not at all. I just laid down. I was still awake. How are you, Peter? How was your day?" I asked.

"Great, actually. I was thinking about you all day and smiling. I am sorry I didn't have a chance to call you earlier, and I am sorry about calling so late. My day kind of got away from me," he explained.

"No worries. Don't be concerned about calling me any time of the day. I was pretty busy at work myself today, and then I had dinner plans with a friend I forgot about, until I got the reminder call from him. When I got home this evening I finished up some stuff around here and just laid down," I said, talking quickly. I was getting anxious again.

"I am not going to keep you. I just wanted to call and say hello and good night," he replied.

"Thanks, that was nice of you. Get some sleep and we can touch base tomorrow." Part statement, part question on my part.

"I will be looking forward to that. Good night, Jeff," he said.

"Good night, Peter," I replied.

With that, I hung up the phone and called it an evening. I drifted off to sleep right away, content. *"He called as he said he would. Life is good."*

We talked almost every day or night from the day we met. It was a great feeling, having made such a great connection with him. We actually enjoyed many of the same things and laughed at the same stuff. Neither one of us took ourselves seriously, so the joking and ribbing we exchanged didn't upset either one of us. He had a great outlook on life, and I loved hearing him talk about his dreams and desires. When he spoke about his family, he spoke with respect, conviction, and pride.

The days seemed to go by slowly, and yet our date night was upon me before I knew it. I had been busy over the weekend with friends in from out of town and other activities. I signed up for bowling and got on a great team. The four other guys were very nice and welcomed me to the team. I did put my disclaimer out there right away. I had not bowled in a few years and it might be some time before I got back up to speed with it, so until I was, I was to be considered the team handicap.

DATE NIGHT

OMG! Tonight was the night. All day at work I was running around getting things done and tying up loose ends. Nothing was going to make me late getting out of there. I couldn't be late. I tried to remain calm and collected. It didn't happen. I was totally wired, all anxious about my first date with Peter.

Nothing bothered me or got in my way. My coworkers knew that something was up, but they weren't sure what it was. Even the three ladies that I was the closest to had no idea what was going on. They tried to pin me down, but I wasn't having it. I didn't have the time, nor did I want to get into the whole thing right then. I love the three of them to death, but in telling them about meeting Peter, I would have been subject to a cross-examination that would rival *Law & Order,* or at the very least *Judge Judy.*

I became a clock-watcher as the end of my workday neared. The last couple of hours seemed to drag by. I finished everything that I needed to finish, and with nothing left on my desk, time stopped. It was frustrating. The phone rang, and the caller ID indicated that it was Peter. My heart sank. There was still time for him to cancel, and I just knew that he was going to.

"Hey, mister," I said, answering the phone.

"I'm sorry, but I have some bad news," Peter said rather soberly.

Trying not to show my disappointment, I replied, "What's that?"

"It seems that I have finished up earlier than I originally thought I would, which means I can pick you up earlier than planned and you have to spend more time with me than you were expecting to," he said.

"Doesn't sound like bad news to me." I let out a sigh of relief.

We discussed a rough timetable and agreed that I would call him when I got home. He was coming in to the city, and that would give me enough time to shower and dress. It was going to be enough time, considering I already had my fashion crisis that morning before leaving for work.

I got home in record time. I hit all the trains and transfers just right. I was actually ahead of schedule. I ran through the shower, after calling him, checked to make sure the condo looked presentable, and made sure everything was in its place. The phone rang and it was him. *"Still time for him to back out,"* I thought as I answered the phone. He reported that traffic was a bit slow and said he would call me when he got closer to my building. *"How sweet was that?"* I thought as we hung up.

His call came, and I headed to the elevator, pushed the button, and waited. The elevator didn't come fast enough, so I pushed the button multiple times, because as everyone knows, doing that makes the elevator arrive quicker. Four elevators in my building and all of them were on other floors. It was a conspiracy to make me late—I was sure of it!

I was waiting out front on the half circle drive when he pulled up. I got an award-winning smile and a quick wave, as his car came to a stop and the passenger side window descended.

"Get in! I have been waiting all day for this," he said.

"Do I know you?" I joked. He just smiled, leaned over his console, and opened my door.

He put the car in gear, and we started off to the restaurant. The conversation started immediately. I sat back in awe, thinking about how easy it was for me to talk with him. I had never been so comfortable with someone so soon after meeting him.

Our reservations were for this small, quaint, hole-in-the-wall place. Everything about it was appealing. We elected to eat outside on the patio. The patio was shaded with table umbrellas and a gigantic oak tree. The tree was in the middle of the patio, and its branches spread the width of the patio on all four sides. Lattice work around the top of the fence was entwined with ivy and assorted flowering vines. There were candles on every table, and they flickered in the light breeze of the evening.

There was no urgency to the evening. It all flowed smoothly. We sat and talked over a drink and took our time in ordering dinner. There weren't a lot of people when we arrived, but soon the place was bustling. It had no effect on Peter and me. Even though there were another forty or fifty people around, it was as if we were alone, by ourselves. All of his attention was directed to me and mine to him.

We spent the evening laughing and talking. He was very easy to be with. He expounded on his thoughts about relationships, one of the tangent subjects we found ourselves on. I found it interesting that his thoughts paralleled mine. He explained that he felt nothing could be forced, that he wanted to wake up some morning and have it just hit him: "I'm in a relationship." He felt it didn't have to be decided or arranged—it just evolved. I was in full agreement.

While we were on the subject, I explained my only dating rule. It is called the six-and-two rule. He laughed pretty hard as I explained it. I actually think he was leading me on and toying with me, when he had me explain it a second time. "It's simple," I said. "I don't have sex with someone until I have either had six dates or we have dated for two months."

I explained myself further, and he agreed that having sex immediately in a relationship sometimes confuses the issues and emotions, that it puts the relationship on a different level. We also agreed that waiting until the time was right made sharing that aspect of a relationship more special.

I paused for a moment and thought, *"Why are we even discussing this? It is only our first date, and who knows if it is going to go any further?"* I decided that it was just the way the conversation was going. We seemed to be touching on so many different subjects, and this was just one of them. We didn't labor on it, and before long we were off on another topic.

He became quiet at one point. I wasn't sure why. The conversation seemed to be going well, and I didn't think I had said anything stupid or offensive. I studied him for a moment and watched as he gathered his thoughts. He was thinking about something. I had seen him do this before. It was in the condo, when he was getting ready to leave, after going up on the roof. He was gathering his thoughts.

"Jeff, want to go for a lake walk after dinner?" he asked.

"Sure. It's one of my favorite things to do," I said.

"That isn't what I wanted to say, but I told you I am not good at this sort of thing at times. Most times," he said, with a hint of frustration.

"OK...what did you want to say?" I asked.

"I wanted to say...ummm...well, it's that I, ah... I am glad that we met and that you agreed to have dinner with me," he said, sighing as if some weight had been lifted from his shoulders.

I looked at him for a moment, realizing that he was probably as anxious about the evening as I was. We were both experiencing the first date jitter stuff. I had an internal fight going on—I was trying not to let my jitters sabotage the evening and he appeared to be having the same struggle.

"Peter, there is no need for you to be anxious about saying anything to me. I am glad we met, too. I have been looking forward to this evening ever since we set it up," I said reassuringly.

"I am just worried that I am going to mess it up," he explained.

"Me, tooooo! I'm worried you're going to totally mess things up also!" I said with a smile. "So, let's just relax a bit. We seem to be managing just fine."

He shot me one of those award-winning, heart-melting smiles I so enjoyed and we got back down to the business at hand, just having a good time.

When dinner was finished and after we'd had an after-dinner coffee, we haggled over the check and I lost. He insisted on paying. He did compromise, however, saying that the next dinner was on me. It was a relief to hear that he wanted to have a second date.

As we walked out of the restaurant, I was cool and calm on the exterior. Internally I was that little kid, screaming, jumping up and down on his bed with excitement, having just scored a second date with him.

We piled into the car and drove to the lake. We actually parked across from my building, where he had parked the day we met. We walked along the pathway to the water. It was very serene and romantic. The moon was full and bright, and it lit the water at the tips of the waves. The whole lake seemed to sparkle and shimmer. There were a few sailboats and other maritime craft out skimming across the water. He told me that his father taught him how to sail and expressed how much enjoyment he got from sailing. He added that he no longer had a sailboat of his own and said he missed it. He was pretty confident that he would own his own sailboat again in the near future.

We stood at the water's edge, just staring out over the water. As we stood there, he stepped in close. We were shoulder to shoulder. As we talked about whatever came to mind, he hesitated slightly, then reached up and put his arm around me. My entire body tingled at his touch. I leaned in slightly, looked up, and smiled. We stood there silently for a few minutes, and then it was time to leave. It was getting late, and he had to drive back home. As much as I didn't want it to end, I knew—we knew—that it had to.

He wouldn't let me walk through the tunnel to my building. It wouldn't be the proper ending to a first date, he told me. It took just a couple of minutes to get from where we were to my building. Pulling into the drive, he stopped the car and put it into park.

He leaned into me and he kissed me. I was fully receptive to it. It was one of the best kisses I had ever had. It rated right up there in the top five, maybe even in the top three. I believe that it all starts with the kiss and if that is true…we were off to a good start. He was tender, gentle, and passionate. He wasn't over the top with it. It was just right. We broke the embrace and kiss, and as we pulled away, we both were just smiling. I reached for the door and said good night, and he watched me exit the car. I stood and waved good-bye.

Off he drove. I wasn't ready to go inside yet. I was still on an endorphin high from the date and decided to take a walk around the block. When I returned to the building, Robert was still on duty and was waiting to greet me. We talked for a short time—Robert wanted details about my date and Peter. Giving him the *Reader's Digest* version of the evening, I said good night and headed to the elevators.

Nothing about the date went wrong—it was about as perfect a date as a date could be. The conversation was good, I didn't embarrass myself, I didn't drop food in my lap, and, most importantly, I didn't say anything stupid. The phone rang as I was getting ready for bed. It was Peter calling to say good night and to tell me that he had a great time. We talked for a short time before saying good night. After we hung up, I was thinking that I liked this guy more and more, and our date this evening only solidified that I wanted to spend more in-person time with him.

The phone rang again.

"Jeff, I really had a good time," he said. "Thanks."

"I had a great time as well. We should do that again," I said, more as a question than a statement, kind of testing the sincerity of his second date comment earlier.

"I agree. Let's talk tomorrow and see how our time looks for the weekend," he responded.

"All right, sounds like a plan. I will talk with you tomorrow, then," I said. He was sincere and I was excited.

"Yep. And, oh, I forgot to ask," he added, pausing before asking devilishly, "Is tonight one of six?"

"It had all the elements of a date. You picked me up. We had dinner and coffee. We went out to the lake. You drove me home and kissed me good night. I suppose we could count it. Yup, it's one of six," I answered.

"SWEET! One down and five to go—and the countdown begins," he said playfully.

"My friends think it is pretty silly, Peter, the six-and-two rule. Are you sure you are all right with it?" I asked.

"Actually I like the idea of taking it slow, as difficult as it might be to keep my distance from you," he responded.

"No one said you had to keep your distance. We just can't do the dirty," I said, laughing.

"Good to know, because I think I like being up close and personal with you. I am off to bed now. I will call you tomorrow," he said.

"Good night, Peter," I replied.

We hung up again and I found myself curled up in the pillow next to me and drifting off to sleep with sweet thoughts of him. I was hoping he was thinking of me as well. Softly and barely audibly, I murmured, "Good night, Peter."

CHAPTER 3

Diving In (the lake date!)

There was little time for the two of us in the next couple of weeks. My schedule held meetings out of town, a camping trip with friends, and other activities that I had committed to. His schedule was just as full, with family and friends and work. We spoke often, during the day and at night. We would compare calendars every time we talked to see if anything had freed up. Nothing did.

I was OK, at least for the short term, with the phone conversations, e-mails, and instant messaging, but I also wanted to see him. I needed to be near him and just touch him, sit beside him and smell him. I wanted to be close to him—so close that you couldn't get a credit card between us. He proclaimed the same to me. We were getting involved; it was getting somewhat serious, I was thinking. How funny—a chance meeting, dinner date, and it turned into an electronic relationship. I would have to settle for that until there was time for us to actually spend time.

At times I actually thought that the electronic and cyberspace relationship we were engaged in was working on our behalf. We were getting to know each other in depth, without the distraction of physical attraction. On the other hand, I needed and wanted to be with him, spending time together. It was going to happen soon, once our schedules let up.

In the couple of weeks that passed, we discovered a variety of things about each other. We had so much in common and shared a lot of the same likes and dislikes. There was always a positive spin on everything. I rediscovered so much about myself while talking with him, and experienced a new awakening. I learned a lot about him. I absorbed everything he told me.

He asked plenty about me. I found myself answering everything with an open and honest approach. I didn't hesitate to answer anything that he might ask. I wasn't my usual reserved and protected self. It was a time of discovery for both of us, and we seemed to be enjoying it. We were going to have some time soon. We tried to make some time to spend time together in person, but it just didn't seem to be happening. It was mainly my schedule that was causing the conflict.

We finally got the time to get another dinner in. One of my commitments cancelled, and I had an evening free. I took the train north, and he met me at the station. We had a great time, and it was good to be with him. He insisted that he drive me home, saying that the more details he could include, the more it would look like a date, which would let him mark another one off the countdown to six.

I said nothing, having already calculated the two-month mark and having written it on my calendar and in my day planner. As he drove, I reached over and laid a hand on his thigh, slowly caressing it as he drove. He reached over and took my hand in his and raised it to his lips. He kissed the back of my hand lightly and laid it back down on his leg.

As we pulled into the drive, I asked if he wanted to come up for a short time. He declined, saying that he had a meeting with a new client in the morning and wanted to get some sleep. He got out of the car with me, took hold of my hand, and reeled me in close. I was a bit concerned about the foot traffic around us, as he kissed me in the middle of the driveway. It didn't seem to concern him, so I didn't let it concern me.

This kiss was even better than the first. It was full of passion, yet it was delivered with a tender gentleness. He had me and he knew it. I was just a marshmallow in his hands. I returned the kiss with all the gusto and passion I had, matching what he was delivering. As we stood there in the embrace, lips locked like there was no tomorrow, the world and time stood still. I was totally unaware of my surroundings. I had to lean up a bit—he was six foot four. *"We fit"* came to mind. It felt right—no pieces were missing in our physical togetherness. I wanted to speed ahead to date six that very moment, but couldn't and wouldn't.

I was in bed when the phone rang, and it was him. He had made a habit of calling me every night. It was a blissful conversation that bordered on pornographic at times. We shared some very intimate details of what we were doing and thinking.

The pitch of our conversation ended in short, seductive sentences, with some very audible moaning. I could feel him caressing my body at times, while we talked. I envisioned him there beside me, taking me into his arms and making love to me. It all started out humorous and lighthearted, but as we played back and forth, the comments became more direct and specific. Our desire for each other was being expressed in a heated verbal assault. An urgency to share the intimacy at that precise moment arose in our voices.

Breathless and spent, we both took a few moments to gather our thoughts before saying anything. What could have been said at that moment, anyway? I wanted to bask in the thought: *"That is what it would have been like if it had truly happened and were not just a phone fantasy."*

"Jeffrey," he spoke first. "That was SWEET and kind of fun."

"Oh, man, tell me about it! I thoroughly enjoyed it, and after that kiss tonight, I needed that," I weakly replied.

He snickered a bit devilishly and promised me that on date six, or the sixty-second day, it would only be better. I was sure it would be. At the moment, I could only imagine what it would be like. I countered with a few promises of my own, each of us making mental notes of what the future would bring, when that time came.

Fully recovered from the climatic conversation, we said our good nights. I wanted to tell him that I was growing extremely fond of him and that I didn't want this to end—whatever THIS was. Whatever it was, I was enjoying it. I stopped short of telling him that, figuring it would be better to tell him in person. When would that be? Our schedules were starting to loosen up and we would have more time together. I was looking forward to that, and yet it was a bit scary.

I wasn't going to let the dating hysteria consume me. I kept telling myself to keep a level head. I listened at times, but others I was off on tangents. Dating just instills self-doubt in all of us. It is human nature to be concerned about what someone thinks of you, especially if that someone is the subject of your desires and dreams. So far, Peter seemed to be that person.

Middle of August in Chicago was living up to years past. It was hot, humid, and oppressive. Good thing it only lasts about two weeks. It was Friday night, and I was walking home from the train. The cell phone rang, and it was Peter. Immediately my spirits soared. He asked where I was and I told him. I also told him I was stopping by the grocery on my way home. We continued to talk as I walked. As I approached the store, I told him I would call him back when I got home.

I entered the store with no idea of what I wanted for dinner. Nothing sounded good because of the heat, and my mind changed several times. I walked the aisles, picked up a few things that I needed, and then concentrated on dinner. Something cool and refreshing was in order. Chilled chicken salad and watermelon was sounding pretty good.

I was standing there looking at the watermelon, and from behind me I heard this sexy velvet voice: "Is there going to be enough for me?"

Resisting the urge to turn around, I responded, "Maybe."

"I think the one on the upper right looks best," he said, reaching forward from behind and handing it to me.

"Thanks. They all looked good," I said.

"Speaking of looking good…" he leaned in and lowered his voice. "You look great!"

"Thanks. You sound great." I hadn't turned to look at him yet. "What are you doing here? I thought you had to work," I said.

"Inviting myself to dinner. My dinner appointment canceled. Please tell me you don't have plans," he said.

"I do." Turning and facing him, I allowed a noticeable pause of a few moments to pass before I continued. "I have this dinner date. It just came up—a last-minute thing…" Trying to remain straight-faced, I let my statement sink in. I could see him processing it. He was a little unsure of what I meant. Then he got it and began to smile.

"SWEET!" was all he said, and we walked and finished shopping for dinner.

The condo was cool, compared to the outdoors. The lake breeze kept the place very comfortable. I didn't usually have to run the air conditioner, but I asked if he wanted it on. He declined and just turned the floor fan on, and that helped even more.

"Let's eat at the lake," he suggested.

"I was thinking along those lines, too. Help me pack dinner and get this stuff into the basket and off we go," I said.

We found a spot that was shaded and had a nice view of the sailboats heading in and out of the harbor. Dinner at the lake was an intimate affair. There were people scattered about, but neither of us noticed any of them, it seemed. We were lost in the small part of the universe that was smiling down upon us. We both talked about sailing and how we enjoyed it—he knew how to sail and shared stories of adventures with his father; I just enjoyed being out on the water as a passenger.

The sun was setting off to the west, leaving the sky burnt orange. The horizon to the east was dark, as night was beginning to fall. We packed up our supplies and walked back to the condo. We did dishes together and put everything away. There was nothing left to do but put some music on and enjoy the remainder of the time we would have to share that evening.

Night had fallen, though the temperature hadn't. The humidity was not as palatable as earlier in the day and evening. A light breeze wafted gently through the open windows. Smooth, romantic jazz filled the room. The night had all the characteristics of a sultry New Orleans evening.

Peter stood at the window. Walking up behind him, I handed him a glass of wine and wrapped my arms around him. We started to sway back and forth, synchronized with the music. In one smooth, fluid move, he turned from the window, set his wine glass on the coffee table next to mine, and faced me.

Our slow, rhythmic swaying evolved into us slow dancing around my living room. My arms were up around his neck, his around my waist. I slowly caressed his neck and ran my fingers through his hair, as he leaned forward and kissed me. We continued to dance in a kissing embrace without saying a word.

The music stopped, but we didn't—at least not for a few minutes. When we broke the embrace, he retreated to the couch. I restarted the music and went to join him. I leaned down before sitting and gave him a soft kiss on the cheek.

With the slightest of voices and my heart pounding, I asked, "Spend the night?"

I backed away to look him straight in the eyes and await his answer. There was an agonizing pause, as he deliberately acted like he was thinking it over. There was a sparkle in his eyes, and his lips turned up into that award-winning smile as he leaned forward.

"I'd love to!" he replied, and I melted.

I moved around, lay down on the couch, and placed my head in his lap. I stared up at him, in awe of how handsome he was. Candlelight mingled with the light filtering in through the windows. The soft glow enhanced his stunning looks. I wanted him, but I had laid the ground rules and I could not compromise them.

It was getting late and we both were fading. It had been a long day for both of us. I noticed that his eyes were fighting to stay open. I got up and blew out the candles, restarted the CD player from the beginning, and reached for his hand.

We went into the bedroom and undressed. We lay there in each other's arms, the rhythm of our breathing slowed, and we softly drifted off to sleep. I woke in the middle of the night, a bit startled. I wasn't used to having someone in my bed with me. I turned and looked at him. He was in a deep slumber, lying on his side with his back to me. I reached over and wrapped my arm around his chest. He fidgeted a little and then grabbed my hand and held it close. We slept the remainder of the night that way.

In the morning, I was up early. I slipped quietly out of bed to shower and brush my teeth before he got up. I made coffee and walked to the window to watch the boats leave the harbor. The sun was just rising in the eastern sky. I cannot see the sun from my place—it just reflects off the windows of the north tower of my building—but I can see the sparkles of sunlight on the lake.

He emerged, saying the coffee smelled good and he needed a cup and a shower. I got him a fresh towel, washcloth, and spare toothbrush. He showered as I fixed his coffee and took it to the bathroom. I slid the shower door open and handed it to him, and he took a sip or two and handed it back. I closed the shower door and left the coffee on the vanity.

He came out of the bathroom with just a towel wrapped around his waist. I couldn't help but stare. My gaze was filled with the splendor of what, in my opinion, was one fine-looking man. Head to toe, he was very easy on the eyes and very desirable. I walked up and kissed him. He needed to get dressed and head home. We had talked about that the night before, so it wasn't a surprise to me when he mentioned it.

"I don't want to dress and leave," he said. "I would rather stay and spend the morning with you."

"I understand you have to. Family is important and you have to be there," I replied.

"Why don't you come along with me? It would be fun," he offered.

"I can't. Remember, I have commitments as well. Soon our schedules will work out and we'll have all sorts of time to share," I said.

"It doesn't make leaving here any easier," he said, as he slid his hands down my back and drew me near.

We stood there for a few minutes in a tender embrace. I broke the embrace and led him by the hand to the window. He stood there looking out the window as I wrapped my arms about his waist. I kissed the back of his neck and just stood there looking at the boats. I left him standing by the window as I gathered our coffee cups and brought them over. We watched the boats gliding effortlessly over the water, in and out of the harbor, while we drank our coffee.

He dressed and said good-bye. We talked on the phone throughout the day and that evening. I was going through my day feeling fulfilled. The evening before had been wonderful, and he spent the night with me. Sleeping with him felt comfortable. We fit together like jigsaw puzzle pieces.

The weekend ended, and we were back to work. I called him from my office that morning and we chatted for a short time. We both had this feeling our days were going to get away from us, and they did.

I took Wednesday off—another mental health day. I had the vacation to burn. One of the perks of my job was the ability to call in last minute and take a vacation day, if staffing permitted. I was still up early, having coffee at my desk while playing on the computer. I read e-mails and talked with cyber friends via instant messenger. I had showered earlier while the coffee was brewing, but hadn't gotten dressed yet. It was warm in the condo that morning, and judging by how warm it was so early, I knew that day would be a scorcher.

I went to refill my coffee cup when my IM program chimed. It was Peter.

> *Peter: Good morning, Jeffrey. Thought you would be at work already.*

> *Me: I took a mental health day. Just having coffee.*

> *Peter: You feeling all right?*

> *Me: Yep, fine. Just wanted to take the day off.*

Peter: Any plans?

Me: Nope, just going to do whatever comes up.

Peter: OK, sounds good. Call you later.

Me: OK, Peter. Have a good day.

The computer conversation was short. I figured he was at work already. I busied myself with things around the house. I was getting domestic things started when the phone rang. Not having caller ID on my bedroom phone, I wasn't sure who was calling. I wasn't expecting anyone to call. Maybe it was the girls from work checking up on me. I answered and was pleasantly surprised to hear Peter's voice.

"Hey, what are you doing?" he inquired.

"Hey, mister. You mean in the past sixty minutes since we were on the computer?" I joked.

"Don't be a smart-ass. It's so unbecoming of you," he jokingly suggested.

"Thanks for the advice. You're right—it is unbecoming. I haven't done much of anything, really," I said.

"Well, I am trying to get an appointment with a guy in your neighborhood. I am in the car and heading that way. Hope he will have time to see me," he said.

"Great. Can we have coffee before you meet with him or lunch afterwards, if you have the time?" I asked.

I was taking a liberty, assuming he would have time or want to play hooky from work. His days were usually pretty busy with work and keeping his company in demand. He was serious about it and dedicated a lot of energy into making it what it was.

"Well, Jeff, I am talking with him right now," he said.

"You are?" I asked a bit confused.

"Yep, I have him on the phone right now," he said.

I didn't catch it when he said it. It didn't sink in. I was thinking he had some potential client on his car phone and was talking with me on his cell. I was a bit astonished by that. I couldn't help but inquire about it.

"So, let me get this straight. You have a guy on the phone and you are on another phone with me? Peter, you are a highly intelligent guy, but how does your company stay in business if you have a potential client on hold and you are talking to me about lunch or coffee?" I asked.

"I didn't say it was a client. I said it was an appointment. I am trying to get an appointment with you, Jeff. You are the guy," he said.

Without missing a beat, I replied, "Well, then, I will have to check my day-timer and calendar and see what I have going on and get back with you."

"You told me earlier your day was open. I will be there in about twenty minutes. Meet me out front," he instructed.

"Where we going?" I asked.

"It's a surprise," he said.

"All right. Twenty minutes it is," I agreed.

I hung up and raced through the house, thinking of what I was going to wear. I had no idea where we were going, and it was getting very warm outside. I put on my favorite shorts and summer shirt. I grabbed a bottle of water, and out the door I went. I arrived outside about the same time he pulled up.

I got into the car, he leaned in and kissed me, and we were off. The destination was still unknown to me. We headed north on Lake Shore Drive and settled into our easy way of conversing. I wanted to know where we were going, but I wasn't going to ask—not just yet, anyway.

We drove for about thirty minutes, and I just had to inquire where we were going. I didn't get an answer. He acknowledged the question, but didn't answer it—at least not with the answer I wanted. I just got the "it's a surprise" answer. I would have to settle for that. It was kind of fun not knowing.

We pulled into a parking lot adjacent to a harbor that moored some of the most beautiful boats I had ever seen. I had never been this far north along the lake. I was unfamiliar with where we were. He had me intrigued and very curious.

We walked through the cars and towards the docks. We arrived at one of the nicest sailboats I had seen. He looked at me and said, "Get on board. We are going for a little sail." I couldn't believe it. We boarded the boat, and he handled everything. He had us untied from the dock and floating freely within minutes. I assisted where I could.

"Whose boat is this? Where are we going?" These were just a couple of the questions that were meandering through my mind. I figured that would all be revealed to me in good time. He had us motoring out of the harbor and into the vast open waters of Lake Michigan. The lake was calm

and there was a mild breeze. As we left the harbor, I became impressed with the way Peter handled the boat and slipped us into our maritime adventure.

He gave me some direction in what to do to help him. He cut the motor and we raised the sail. He seemed so at ease, raising the sail, navigating us out into open water, and entertaining me all at the same time. The brightly colored sail captured the breeze and powered the craft into the open water. It wasn't that windy out, and the lake was calm, so we slowly sailed away from the harbor. There was a slight yaw and pitch, but the lake was so calm, it was barely noticeable.

I finally asked him whose boat it was and how he got this all set up. When did he have time to get this master plan into play? He explained that after he found out that I didn't have to work, he took the day off and called his best friend Bill, who owned the boat. In the time between our computer conversation and his phone call, Bill and Peter managed to get the boat ready and stock it with some supplies in the cabin below. Peter explained that not much prep work was needed; Bill keeps the boat pretty well stocked and ready to go, for impromptu occasions like this.

Bill was Peter's best friend, long-time family friend, and lawyer. They grew up together, went to college together. They were business partners at some point for a short time, until the business took off and they sold it. You could tell that Peter respected and sincerely liked his buddy.

It was pure joy sailing that morning with the guy whom I was beginning to fall for—OK, already fell for. I wasn't in love—it was just heavy like. I sat there watching him command the boat with such expertise. I know nothing about sailing, and was smitten enough with him that he could have been making a thousand mistakes and I wouldn't have known. I looked back at the shoreline and harbor, shrinking from view. I didn't know how far out we were, but I knew I couldn't swim back if I had to.

I had not known Peter that long—less than two months—and there we were out in the middle of Lake Michigan. No one knew that I was out there with him. I didn't have the time to call anyone. OK, I neglected to call anyone. Was that by design, part of his master plan? A couple of thoughts popped into my head—*"I'm shark bait"* was one of them. OK, we were in fresh water, and the chances of a great white devouring me were nil, but it still popped into my head. My next thought was Jimmy Hoffa, complete with the visual of cement slippers and the slow spiral down through the water to the lake bottom. Ted Bundy, *The Texas Chainsaw Massacre, Friday the 13th,* and all the "B" slasher movies quickly whizzed through my head. I really didn't have those kinds of gut feelings about him. My instincts told me that I could trust him, and I had learned to trust those feelings. They had never failed me in the past.

He was easygoing about our morning sail. He talked about when he was younger and his father and he would go out sailing together and their sailing adventures. I could tell that he missed having a boat of his own. I was happy to sit there, listen to the stories, and watch as he maneuvered the boat through the water. Soon we were where he wanted to be, and he asked me to help lower the sail and anchor.

"We have reached our destination," he said to me, and he moved around and secured the sail.

"We have? I could have sailed around all morning—all day for that matter," I said, almost pouting.

"We still have the sail back. I just thought we would anchor here and enjoy the lake and the abundance of sunshine," he answered.

"It's so relaxing. I can see why you love it and miss it so much," I commented.

"I really do. I packed some water in the cooler for us, a couple of beach towels. I'll go below and get them," he said.

"How sweet. You thought of everything," I replied.

"My only thought was to spend time with you today. When I found out you were off, the rest fell into place," he said, heading below.

Returning with the cooler, two large beach towels, and a couple of other things, he threw a couple of smaller towels on the seat next to me and then motioned for me to follow him to the forward deck. We spread out and anchored the huge beach towels, cracked open a couple of bottles of water, and sat down.

There were no other boats around. It seemed as if we were isolated out on the lake, just the two of us bobbing slowly on the rolling movement of the water. The conversation continued as we shared thoughts and ideas. We talked about our pasts and different events that happened to us along the way. Peter produced a tube of number forty-five sunblock. I am very fair skinned, so I burn easily. Just thinking about going out in the sun for any length of time usually generates a sunburn for me. I told him that my summer is usually spent in a cycle of pasty white, lobster red, peeling, and pasty white. I thanked him for the sunblock and applied a generous amount to my arms, legs, and face.

We were talking about nothing and everything at the same time, when he announced that it was time to take a swim to cool off. It caught me off guard and unprepared, and I told him as much. I watched as he stood and removed his shirt and stuffed it into a mesh bag that was anchored with the towels.

"I didn't bring a suit either, Jeff," he admitted calmly.

With that, he turned, surveyed the horizon in all directions, undid his shorts, and let them drop to the deck. He stood there in his bright white briefs for a second, hooked his thumbs under the waistband, and in one swift, flowing move removed them.

I had seen him naked before, the evening he spent the night. I was still totally taken back by how stunning he was standing there. He was perfect in my eyes, and I was so enamored with him. His shoulders were broad, and there was a noticeable V shape from his upper torso to his waist. His butt was nicely shaped—round and firm and yet not rock solid. There was a slight covering of dark hair that only got thicker on his thighs and legs. I was staring at him as he stood there looking out over the water. I couldn't help it, I couldn't stop it, and I didn't want to, either.

"Now you have done it. You've taken off all your clothes and expect me to as well. I don't look good in this harsh lighting," I joked, as his back was still to me.

A slight breeze blew up, and I watched the hair on his thighs shift back and forth. I was getting aroused and excited just staring at him. I couldn't stop it or help myself. He was just so beautiful. He turned to face me and I felt faint. I couldn't let my eyes drop below his waist. I might have lost all self-control if I had! His chest was defined—not gym workout defined, but in a way that nature had gifted him with. The spray of dark hair that covered his chest thinned some on his abs. The light covering of hair on his abs fanned out towards his sides. There was a pronounced treasure trail, leading from his navel south to his groin, but I didn't allow myself to follow it.

I set the guidelines—six dates or a minimum of two months of dating, but my resistance was getting weak just looking at him. I tried to remain calm and composed, but that was getting difficult.

"Hey, you going to join me here for a swim?" he invited, breaking my gawking trance.

"Yeah, but if you think you can bring me out to the middle of the lake, so far that I can't swim back, get me naked, and have your way with me..." I sarcastically began to say.

He interrupted with a smirk. "I know, I know. It's that six-and-two thing. I have three more dates, and by my count, I have fifteen days to go. This is just enjoying ourselves. Come on, it will be a blast," he encouraged.

He turned quickly and over the side he went. I quickly stripped off my clothes and followed him into the water. I didn't want my obvious excitement to be exposed. The cool temperature of the lake water would take care of my condition. *"HOLY SHIT!"* my mind screamed as I sliced through the water. Diving overboard, you cut through the warmer surface water and the deeper you plunge, the colder the water gets. The layer of warm surface water seemed very thin at that moment.

We swam around for about fifteen or twenty minutes. I came around behind him and pressed the full length of my body against his. I embraced him, wrapping my arms around his chest and curling my legs around his thighs. A slight shiver ran through my body. He turned and took me in his arms. We began to kiss passionately, trying to remain buoyant. We were close to the boat—he held me with one arm while holding onto the diving platform on the stern of the boat.

"That was invigorating," he said, as he broke away and hoisted himself up on the platform. He sat there looking at me and then pointed down to his groin and began to laugh. "I am only half the man I was before diving in."

I swam up between his dangling legs and rested my arms on his lower thighs, just above the knees. I was half in and out of the water and eye level with his groin.

"Half looks pretty nice from where I am," I answered with a diabolical smile.

"Haul yourself out of there, dry off, and warm up a bit in the sun with me," he said.

He moved from the center of the platform to give me room to maneuver. I anchored my hands on the platform, sank down in the water a bit, came up with a half twist, and landed right next to him. It was a perfectly executed gymnastic move of Olympic quality.

He handed me a towel to dry off with. The sun's warmth had already started to dry my skin and hair. The heat felt great in contrast to the chilly water of the lake. What the sun's rays didn't evaporate, the warm breeze did. We were both dry in minutes.

We sat there looking out at the lake and how vast it was. I placed my hand on the inside of his thigh and gave it a pat. I kept my hand on his thigh, and it rested there comfortably. He brought his hand to mine, and we sat there holding hands and staring at the beautiful day we were sharing.

We moved off the platform to the forward deck where we had started. We didn't dress. We just lay on the beach towels and soaked up the sun. I leaned over, kissed him, and rolled onto my stomach. I was looking into his dark brown eyes that danced with life. I broke out into a huge grin. As I reached for his hand, our fingers became entangled.

"I could get used to this and you," I said. It was in my head and out my mouth before I could stop it.

"Good," he replied, smiling back at me.

He turned on his side and faced me. He started to caress my back and butt. His very touch sent shock waves through my entire body. I don't think there was a single molecule in my body that didn't become more alive and start to tingle. I turned to face him, and he ran his hand down my shoulder and arm. I, in return, mirrored his actions.

A light kiss on the lips, and he grinned and stared at me. Never removing his gaze from mine, he simply repeated his response of just a moment ago: "Good."

He wrapped his arms around me and brought us closer. Our bodies were alive and excited. It felt as though every cell and inch of me was on fire. I could feel the full length of his hardness against mine. There was no way to hide my excitement and desire for him. He wasn't trying to hide his for me. His hands were exploring my back and torso. They came to rest in the small of my back and just held me tight.

I ran my fingers through his hair and around to the back of his head. I guided his face closer to mine and kissed his cheek, as I lay back against the deck with his face angled above me. I ran my tongue lightly across his lips. He reacted to my advances, and his breathing became a bit labored, as did mine. Our movement stopped and he looked down at me.

"We can't continue with this," he said with a smile, adding, "or I will be forced to finish it. There are the dating rules, remember?"

"I remember the damn things. What was I thinking when I came up with that silly policy?" I said with a little frustration.

"I respect that you have them and they are part of who you are. So maybe another dip to cool off would be a good thing," he suggested.

He knelt facing me and extended his hand. His erection was softening slowly and his testicles were loosening and lowering. The excitement level between us was diminishing.

He was beautiful, simply beautiful. I rose up onto my knees and faced him. I brought one hand up and laid it flat on his chest. I slowly ran it down to his waist, never losing eye contact with him.

He moaned softly as my hand continued its journey. I brought my hand down between his legs and rested it on the inside of his thigh. The back of my hand brushed against his scrotum. I felt it retract and react as I kissed him passionately.

"I don't mean to tease or taunt you. I find it very difficult to keep my hands off of you. I want us to be sure of where we are going before we take this child's play any further," I said with frustration.

He caressed my back and touched me tenderly. His experienced hands had me fully excited in a matter of minutes, as we knelt facing each other. We were sharing an innocent moment of bliss. He moved his hands to my buttocks and held me tight.

"I don't mind waiting. I really don't. I want to be sure as well. I just want to be close to you like this. I want to feel you and smell you and taste you. I just want to be this close to you every time we are together. I want us to share in our mutual admiration of one another. We don't have to have sex—not yet, and not until it is the right time. I don't want this to end, though. I want to be like this every time we are together," he said. He spoke with such clarity and sincerity.

Standing up, he took my hand, saying nothing. I stood there holding his and just looked into his eyes. He led us to the edge of the boat, and we jumped into the water together. The cool water again took care of the evidence of our physical excitement. After swimming for a few minutes and enjoying a little more horseplay, we were back on the platform on the aft end.

As we dried ourselves off, he said, "We need to get some clothes on you—you are starting to burn."

"I always do. Can't get away from it," I said with exasperation.

As I bent forward to reach for my underwear, he leaned in and kissed the small of my back, and a soft moan escaped. I wanted to give in so badly. I wanted to share everything with him. He wrapped his arms around me and pressed his body against mine as he kissed up my back and to the back of my neck.

I stood and turned to face him. He took the garments from my hand and shook them out. He leaned down and spread them out for me to step into.

Placing my hand on his shoulder to steady myself, I stepped into my briefs. He slowly slid them up my legs. When he got to mid-thigh, he hesitated a moment and kissed the inside of each of them.

The touch of his lips and darting tongue sent quivers up my spine. My hands were entwined in his hair. My head fully extended back and my eyes closed tightly. The pleasure of this simple gesture was driving me to my limits of self-control. His movements were so tender and soft. I was on the edge of giving in.

He finished raising my briefs up over my hips, and I adjusted myself for comfort. We were facing each other and just smiled. He was getting dressed along with me. He was an incredible sight, in or out of clothing.

"That was just a preview of the things to come and what I want to do to you and with you," he said.

"I'm sorry, it seems a bit cruel and hateful of me to…"

He stopped me mid-sentence with two fingers against my lips and kissed my forehead. He told me he could wait and wanted to as well. He went on to tell me that he enjoyed the sensuality and playfulness we shared. When the time was right, we would know and we would give ourselves completely to each other. I was becoming the weak one, it appeared, and they were my rules.

It appeared that we were on the same page with things and heading in the right direction. We agreed that we didn't want to force anything. We both wanted our next relationship to evolve naturally. I told him I just wanted to wake up one day and realize that I was in a relationship, not think about it and plot it out to make it happen. It was feeling like things were getting serious between us. I was enjoying those thoughts, and it appeared as though he liked those thoughts, too. It was a feeling I had. We didn't have an in-depth conversation on the boat or that day, but I was sensing it.

We needed to get back to shore and into the harbor. We both had engagements to attend. Reluctantly, we started gathering our belongings and stowed them away, raised the sail, and ventured back in. The sail back was as enjoyable as the sail out.

While securing everything down, once we arrived back into the slip, I was trying to convince him to drop me off at the train to save him some time. He wouldn't even consider that suggestion. Jokingly, he said that if he dropped me off at the train, it wouldn't be counted as a date. He smiled one of those award-winning smiles, with a hint of devilishness added. He confessed the real reason was just to spend a little extra time with me.

I think it was at that moment that I really considered that I might be falling in love with this man. Granted, it had been mainly an electronic and cellular relationship up to this point, with a couple of actual dates thrown in, but I was feeling and thinking things that I hadn't in a long time.

"Damn, you are red. I think I might have kept you out there tooooooo long, Jeff," he said.

"You didn't keep me out there against my will. Am I that red? It doesn't feel that way," I said. I inspected my arms and stomach. "Yep, I am red. I think the big peel is in my future."

CHAPTER 4

Defining the Undefinable

As he drove me home, he seemed pensive—or maybe I was just imagining it. I hadn't seen him in such a quiet mood before. He started a conversation almost as soon as that thought entered my mind. He again told me that waiting was not an issue with him, the intimacy was important, and he separated sex from sensuality and intimacy. He told me that he wanted to be as close to me as we were that afternoon, or closer. Taking our relationship to the physical would be the next step and it would happen when it was time.

Yep, it was getting serious and I was more than OK with that.

He had a vision of us and the relationship that might be forming between us. He went on to tell me that our paths crossed for a reason and that may not be clear right now to either of us, but there was a reason. I didn't say anything in return. It wasn't the time to reply. I understood exactly where he was coming from. He didn't say anything specific about his feelings; it was general in nature. It might have been a bit guarded. I wasn't sure.

I did know that I was on the same page with him. I also felt the connection between us; however, it was going to manifest itself. I knew my feelings and affection for him were growing and bordering on falling in love with him. I wasn't sure I was ready to surrender completely to it. I was in that confusing stage of dating, and I think he was struggling with that as well.

I took in every word as I sat there quietly. I committed to memory everything he said. I wanted to blurt out that I thought there was a chance I was starting to fall in love with him. That thought was there.

Memories of past relationships filled my head and scared me into silence. He didn't use the word *love* and I wasn't going to be the first, at least not at this point. We really hadn't known each other for that long, but it also felt as if we had known each other for an eternity. Maybe that was the scary part.

My mind was reeling. I had this battle going on inside my head. Should I be up front and honest? Should I just lay it out for him and tell him all the thoughts I was having? Should I remain silent and see where his thoughts were taking him?

I was excited about the possibilities, conflicted with what I was feeling, and confused about how to approach it all. I had a habit of saying things without thinking them through and having them come out all wrong and stupid. I was protecting myself from that as well. I decided to remain silent about my feelings for the time being. I would have my opportunity and know when the time was right.

I wasn't getting an expression of love from him, or was it there and I was missing it? Was I missing something in his statements, due to the conflicts waging war in my brain at that moment? Was he putting thoughts out there to see how I would react? I remained quiet and allowed him to purge his thoughts.

He went on to say that he thought about me all the time and that it was important to him to find time to spend with me. He was getting tired of the phone and computer side of our relationship and felt we needed to have more time together. He stated that he thought that if we were going to give whatever this was between us a chance, we needed that time.

He stopped talking, and the silence was unnerving. He then asked a string of very direct and unavoidable questions.

"So, what do you think? Am I alone here? Where do you see this going? Am I being silly thinking about this stuff too soon? And…"

I cut him off before he could hurl any more questions my way. "I'm not sure. No. I'm not sure. No, you aren't." Looking at me a bit puzzled, he responded, "What?"

I smiled at him, reached over and put my hand on his thigh, and squeezed it. He laid his hand on mine and gave it a strong squeeze. He held it firmly for a moment and asked what I meant. I simply replied that I answered his questions in the order that he asked them. He smiled and hit the rewind button in his head, back to the questions he had asked.

"I did throw a lot at you right then, didn't I?" he sheepishly suggested.

"Yeah. It is the way you feel and I am glad you told me," I replied.

"But?"

"No buts. It is just that we are coming up on my building and that gives me little or no time to answer," I simply explained.

"Maybe that was the way I planned it—apprehensive about how you may answer," he responded.

"Peter, you don't have anything to be apprehensive about. I welcome the opportunity to discuss this. It is just that I tend to get my words all jumbled up and say stupid things when I blurt out replies, especially to questions like that and your thoughts," I explained. I continued, "You haven't scared me away. I think we are on a level playing field here with what we think and feel. I know that after spending time with you today, I want to spend more. I also feel that even though this is all pretty new for us, we need to explore and allow whatever is going to evolve to evolve and be open to the opportunity."

"That makes me feel better. I am not that good with this sort of thing, either. Never have been. I know how I feel and am beginning to feel about you, and I am not sure I want that to pass me or us by," he said.

"Peter, I think we are both in the same place here. We are at that uncomfortable stage and time. Neither of us knows what is going to happen here and where this might take us. We are both being a bit cautious and protective about our feelings and thoughts. We will have the opportunity to talk more. Does that make sense?" I asked.

"It does," he answered.

"Good, because we just missed my building. We will have to continue this another time," I said.

We circled the block and pulled into the U-shaped drive. I just smiled at him, and we embraced. The embrace led us to a kiss, and in the middle of that, another car pulled in behind us. I exited the car, leaned into the passenger side window, and said good-bye.

"I will call you later after I get home this evening," I said.

"What are you doing this evening?" he asked.

"Dinner with Michael and Jodi," I answered.

"Yeah, yeah, yeah, I remember now. I am heading to work to check in with them, and then I'm off to my dinner meeting. Talk with you later," he said.

"Bye," I said.

"See you." Peter flashed me a smile and took off.

I was heading up in the elevator, after a playful and enjoyable conversation with Robert, the doorman. I entered the condo and quickly pulled out clothing to wear that evening. It was mid to late afternoon and I still had time to take a power nap. I stripped out of my clothes and looked in the bathroom mirror. I was red—really red. Peeling was definitely in my future.

———————

Peter and I continued to talk on the phone every day. Our schedules seemed to be working against us, in the short term, anyway. I got to spend a little time with him that weekend. It was short but it was quality.

I took another vacation day at the last minute and surprised him with lunch at his office. I had called and spoken with Patsy and told her what I had planned. I asked her to stall him, if he was going to go to lunch. She assured me that he usually ate at his desk and skipped lunch away from the office. She questioned me about who I was and I told her. I didn't know at the time, but she was not only an employee, but a good friend of Peter's as well. I didn't know that he confided in her and she knew all about me. It was my pleasure to meet her when I got there.

It was a total surprise to Peter when I walked into the office, and I got the opportunity to take a tour and meet the staff. We left pretty abruptly, as he didn't have a lot of time. There was some very important meeting that afternoon that he had to prepare for and, as he put it, be on top of his game.

It was Thursday night, and I arrived home from work a bit late. I had an afterwork event that I was required to attend. My whole body itched from the peeling. I was soaking in everything I could get my hands on, but nothing worked. I just wanted to get out of my clothes, jump into the shower, and nylon scrubby or luffa sponge my entire body, to remove a couple of layers of dead skin.

I was about to step into the shower when the phone rang. I wasn't going to answer it, but did, without looking at the caller ID.

"Hey, what are you doing?" Peter asked.

"I was about to step into the shower and strip away a couple layers of dead skin. Envious?" I joked.

"I am not exactly sure how I feel about that. I have taken a liberty here," he said. He sounded a bit strange.

"Really? What might that liberty be?" I inquired.

"I'm coming over. Actually, I am pulling into the garage now," he said.

"Really?! I guess I will wait to take that shower. Come on up. I'll get dressed," I said.

"I'll scrub your back. I will be up in a minute," he replied, then hung up.

I quickly threw on a pair of shorts and a shirt. I surveyed the house for anything that might be out of place or I might have just thrown out of the way. I didn't have the time to straighten up like I wanted to, but the place was in pretty good shape. There was a knock at the door. I greeted him and let him pass by me. "What a nice surprise," I said.

"Still looking as red as the other day. The peeling isn't as bad as I thought it would be," he said.

"I think I have peeled enough skin to cover another person. How was Austin? Too bad you couldn't have picked the city for that unexpected meeting. Austin is so hot this time of year," I commented, closing the door behind us.

"We will talk about that, and that is kind of why I am here. Let's get you scrubbed and moisturized, and we can get to that," he responded. I could tell something was troubling him.

I got into the shower. Peter didn't join me. I got the scrubby ready, with moisturizing soap, when he opened the shower door. He had changed into a pair of boxers and tank top. He grabbed the scrubby and proceeded to work in a circular motion, from my shoulders to my lower back. I tried to make small talk, not knowing what his pensive mood was about and why he was not really responsive.

When my shower was finished, I dressed and headed out into the living room. He was at the windows gazing out at the boats on the lake. He looked upset and maybe even anxious.

"What is it, Peter?" I asked as I walked to his side.

"We will get to that later. I spread a towel out on the bed. Let's get you moisturized with a layer of lotion on that sunburn," he said.

He gently smoothed on the moisturizer. He left a thin layer of lotion on my back, allowing it to soak in. He would work a little in and then let it set to absorb, repeating this several times. He rolled me over and repeated the process.

I knew him well enough to know that something was weighing heavily on his mind and occupying his thoughts. Something was bothering him. I tried again to make small talk, and that was all I got in return. He wasn't ready to share with me, whatever it was. I just needed to be patient and it would come.

When he was sufficiently satisfied that I was properly oiled, creamed, and moisturized, he got up and started to put the bottles away in the hallway closet. I put some light clothing on and joined him in the living room.

I made some coffee at his request. When it was done, we settled onto the couch. I was becoming worried. What could it be? What could have happened out of town? What did it have to do with me? Something told me that I was about to find out.

He said nothing at first and grabbed my hand. He entwined our fingers and gripped them tightly. His grip was deliberate and strong. It felt like he was holding on for dear life and never wanted to let go. I remained quiet and just looked at him. I could see it in his eyes. It was coming. He was about ready to talk.

It was welling up inside of him, and his eyes gave him away. They were darting everywhere in the room and not focusing on me. He avoided looking at me. He was alert and extremely aware that it was a little uncomfortable for me. That being said, it was still his time frame we were dealing with. He was putting everything he wanted to say in order and was methodically rehearsing how he was going to say it.

He opened his mouth to say something and quickly looked away. He was still formulating his thoughts. I felt that it was going to be any time now. I was preparing myself for the unknown announcement or information. I didn't know what I was preparing myself for—how could I? I didn't have a clue what was going on in his head.

The appointment in Austin had gone well. We spoke every day and he didn't say anything about any problems or concerns. He didn't elaborate on what the meeting was about, and I didn't ask very many questions. If he wanted me to know all about it, he would have told me or, I thought, he would tell me when he got home.

"You weren't part of the plan!" he blurted. I didn't see it coming.

"OK, what plan? I didn't know there was a plan," I answered.

He looked at me and started to speak. I saw what I hadn't noticed before. Sadness. My heart ached immediately. What was this about? What was this plan? Did I miss something? Was I so wrapped up in the newness of our blossoming relationship that I didn't see something?

I maneuvered myself into the corner of the couch, laying one leg along the back of the couch and hanging the other off the front. I nudged him around so that his back was against my chest and stomach. I engulfed him in my arms and just held him for a moment and rested my head on his shoulder, in the nape of his neck.

"When you are ready," I whispered.

He encircled my arms with his and held on tightly. His head was tilted back, nestled up against mine. His eyes were closed. I felt a drop of moisture on my arm. I glanced down and back up. I saw that there was a tear trail down his cheek and a couple more tears welling up in his eyes.

"Peter, what is it? I am becoming very concerned here," I said, gently kissing the nape of his neck.

"Not as concerned as me," he murmured.

"Talk to me. Tell me what has you hurting so. What has you so scared? Is it your family? Is it your health? Did something happen in Austin?" I asked, beginning to feel panicked.

A few minutes passed in silence. He appeared to be collecting himself and his thoughts.

"Yeah, something happened. Let's switch to wine. Coffee is not doing it for me right now. I'll get it for us," he said, fidgeting.

Having said that, he rose from the couch, turned, and looked down at me. He paused for a second and then leaned down and kissed my forehead. I heard the wine being opened, glasses clinking, and a moment later he returned with the wine for us. He poured the wine and then sat in front of me. He sat cross-legged and facing me. His gaze pierced my very being. Whatever this was, I could tell that it was very important to him and he wasn't taking it lightly.

He finally spoke, and it was like the floodgates opened. I sat and listened. I was absorbing every word. I was so tense that my muscles hurt. My mouth was dry. I was being held captive by his words. Neither of us drank our wine. He spoke calmly, deliberately, and with conviction.

"You were not part of the plan," he repeated. I sat mute, returning his undivided attention and gaze.

He explained that he had an opportunity to sell his business. It was a very lucrative offer, one he would be a fool to refuse. There were two companies in Austin and one in Raleigh that were bidding on it. The offers from Austin were much better all around, he explained. He went on to explain each offer in depth to me. I started to understand his quandary, at least the professional side of it. I was still a bit unsure where I fit in.

The two bids from Austin were impressive. The second offer, the one he said he had to seriously consider, seemed to be the best. The offering price for his business was more than he would have imagined. There would be moving expenses, a five-year contract, signing bonuses, and a title. He would be a VP of something or other and a partner. I momentarily stopped listening when he mentioned moving.

He went on to say it was everything that he had been working for. It was everything that he wanted and desired professionally. There was one catch, and that was me. I didn't know how or why that could be. I wasn't focusing on that and was a bit confused. I had a couple hundred questions, but remained silent. He needed to finish his thoughts and explanation.

When he finished telling me everything, I was looking at him inquisitively. I have never had a poker face. What I am thinking and feeling is usually written all over my face. I was trying hard to be stone faced, but I don't think it was working. He picked up on that immediately. Reaching over, he held both of my hands in his.

"So you see, Jeff, you weren't part of the equation. I can't say I am in love with you, but I have very strong feelings and know in my soul that there is a connection between us. I know as time increases between us, I will be in love with you. That is why this is so difficult for me. That is why you are part of this. What I have and feel with you, I have not had with anyone else before," he said.

"I can't be part of this. I can't and won't be the one who stands between you and your life dream. NO! Peter, it can't be that way. I cannot be a deciding factor," I insisted.

"Jeff, it is too late for that. You are a part of this, and there is nothing that can change that. I have become involved and, on some level, emotionally invested with you and what we share. I know it is early, too soon, maybe, but I have to consider you in this decision. It is a feeling that I have, an instinct, call it what you will. I have to follow those feelings as well and at least consider what they are telling me," he frankly said.

"Peter, as flattering as that is and as insightful as your thoughts and statements are, you still can't allow me to be an influence in this decision," I protested.

It took a moment or two for the impact of that exchange to sink in for the two of us. We both were digesting what we had heard and said. Emotions continued to remain high as we sat there looking at each other. My mind was reeling. The first thought was to ask why this was happening. I found a wonderful guy, who I was sure would be my life partner, given a chance.

I was being selfish with my thoughts. I needed to concentrate on what Peter was feeling and thinking. He seemed to be so torn up about the whole situation. I was in the middle of it, from his point of view, anyway.

I watched and listened some more. I knew he was a sensitive man. I was seeing it firsthand. He wasn't being melodramatic about it. He was very sincere. He felt very deeply about his situation and its effect on us.

Our conversation resumed. We debated what my part of all this was and what importance it should have. We were not agreeing about it. My position was that I should not have anything to do with the decision. His was that because of his feelings for me, I was part of it. I played a big part in it. I explained that I couldn't be responsible for him not following his dreams.

He is a deeply sensitive man. He cared about how it would affect his family, his employees, and me. He became methodical again in his talking it through. At one point, he became excited about the future and the possibilities these offers held for him. It was bittersweet for him.

We talked until 1:00 in the morning, and he looked exhausted. I felt exhausted. Somewhere along the way, we did agree that I would not be a factor in the decision. That was the way it needed to be. This was about him and needed to be only about him. These were opportunities that he needed to give his complete attention to professionally, and our relationship, whatever it was or would become, could not be a factor in the decision. We would have to work the details of that out after the professional decision was made.

I tried to suppress a yawn, but it didn't go unnoticed. I would have showered and brewed coffee and stayed up all night for him, if that is what he needed. The evening was getting to him as well and he was reaching his exhaustion point, mentally and physically. We were quiet for a moment; then he broke the silence.

"I took a second liberty this evening," he confessed.

"What might this second liberty be?" I quipped.

"I brought a change of clothes for the morning. They are in the gym bag. Is that all right with you?" he asked.

"More than all right," I said. I placed a hand on the side of his face and continued, "Let's go to bed."

We cleared the things off the coffee table and took them into the kitchen, swapping positions in front of the counter. We got everything put away or at least organized on the counter, glasses and coffee cups in the sink. The evening had taken its toll on him.

"Leave that for the morning," I said, patting his arm.

"All right," he said. "Are you sure?"

"I am sure. We are both tired. Let's get to bed," I said.

We walked from the kitchen to the bedroom. I reached for his hand. He stopped just inside the bedroom and turned to face me. I slipped both hands under his shirt and lifted it over his head. He raised his arms and I removed his shirt. He stood there motionless, eyes closed as I slid his boxers down. He stepped out of them, then stood there watching me strip out of my clothing.

We simultaneously sidestepped, each put one knee on the bed, and lowered each other onto the mattress. I rolled him onto his stomach and started to massage his back. His breathing fell into a heavy rhythm, and he was asleep in a matter of minutes. I slid up next to him, laying an arm across his lower back, and fell asleep as well.

When I awoke, I felt more relaxed than I had the night before. He was still in bed, so I wasn't sure how he would be feeling or if there was going to be any residual fallout from our somewhat intense conversation the night before. I quietly made my way out of the bedroom, started the coffee brewing, took my shower, and was preparing my cup when I heard him enter the kitchen. I took a step or two towards him, and he held his hand up like a school crossing guard, instructing me to stop.

"I haven't gargled, brushed, and showered yet," he warned.

"You know where the stuff is. I will get you a cup of coffee as soon as it is done," I replied.

"Sweet," he answered, turning and walking down the hall.

I prepared his coffee and headed into the bathroom. I slid the shower door open and handed it to him. He took a sip or two and gave it back. I put the cup on the vanity and went to get mine.

"Peter, I was thinking..." I began.

"Jeff, we discussed it enough last night. Let's give it a rest today and digest it all and we will have an opportunity to talk more another time. I am not finished trying to convince you to see my side of this if this deal goes through. I am sure some sort of arrangement can be made," he said.

"That is all fine and good, Peter, but I was thinking we could have breakfast and coffee on the roof deck this morning. What do you think?" I asked.

"Oh, sorry. That sounds great. We will have to dress, though. I am willing to make the sacrifice if you are," he said playfully.

"It is a sacrifice that will have to be made. There aren't going to be many more bright and warm mornings left before fall and winter arrive," I offered.

"All right," he replied, shutting off the shower. "I love you and the way you think."

There it was again. Last night it was thrown out there as a maybe and an uncertainty. Today, this morning, it was being said as a matter of fact. How do I respond? What should I do?

I was on autopilot, it seemed, as I walked to the open shower door, where he was drying off. I stared him directly in the eyes and told him that I loved him also. I did—I knew I did. I had been awake thinking about it off and on last night in bed. I had thought about it while I watched him sleep. It was in the open now. Maybe it would be taken lightly, or maybe it was meant lightly by him. I didn't know. I did know how I felt, and at some point I was going to have to tell him. So I did.

He stood there looking back at me, without any emotion in his eyes. It seemed like an eternity, as the seconds ticked away. Then he broke into an enormous smile and winked at me. He said nothing, just winked. The smile said it all. I said nothing, just turned and walked out, smiling from ear to ear.

Coffee on the roof deck, with a full view of the lake and city, was just spectacular. Our time there was limited, since we both had to be at work that morning. We stood watching the morning sunrise above the eastern horizon, while the morning breeze cloaked us in a sense of serenity. It was a sharp contrast to the emotions of the prior evening. There was no talk of the pending sale of his company or his moving.

I stood there thinking about the information and details he had laid out the evening prior, feeling conflicted. He was in deep thought as well. It was early in our relationship, and some might consider it silly for us to be so distraught. I think it was because of the strong bond and deep spiritual connection that developed and we each felt. It was intangible and yet it was so real for the both of us. It was this intangible something that was causing the problem for him and making me feel so unsettled about the whole thing.

We were standing side by side looking off to the east as I moved in to make physical contact with him. We had our coffee in our hands, standing at the railing in silence. I leaned my head against his shoulder, and he tilted his head to lay it against mine. I am sure he was thinking about the conversation that we had the night before, and I couldn't shake it out of my head.

I had to admit that I was a bit angry as well. I wasn't angry with him about the magnificent opportunity he had just been offered. I was angry that here was a man I was sure was supposed to be in my life for a lifetime and it was all going to be taken away. What about my magnificent deal involving Peter? I felt a bit selfish for what I was thinking.

But I tried to put it all in perspective. The deal wasn't final or a given. He may decide not to accept the offer. I enjoyed brief internal smiles, thinking the deal may not go through. Professionally, it would be a bad decision for him, but he might decide not to. I made up my mind that I wasn't going to allow this to complicate everything. I would have to deal with whatever happened, as it happened.

Little was said as we watched the sunrise, and yet we communicated volumes with our silence. We were both deep in thought about the news he broke the night before. The reality of having to go to work interrupted our sunrise watching. We went back to the condo and got ready for our day. He dropped me off at the train and said good-bye. A train arrived almost immediately after I stepped on the platform, and my phone rang. It was Peter, confirming our plans for that evening. We debated about whether I was going to take a train up to his house or he was going to come and get me. I was firm about taking the train, and he conceded.

CHAPTER 5

V.I.P.'s and Surprises

I put in two days of work in an eight-hour period, or so it seemed. I was a clock-watcher that day. My anxiousness didn't go unnoticed by my three best friends at work. The ladies were very inquisitive. They knew about Peter, but they hadn't met him yet. They wanted details of what was going on.

We seemed to take time every day, no matter how busy we were, to gather and catch up on what was going on. They are some of my most treasured friends and core support group. We are all in tune with one another. There are times when saying nothing speaks volumes. We instinctively know when something is going on with one of the others in our clique.

Gwen is the matriarch of the group and office. A beautiful woman, her life is rich and full with family and friends. She has an abundance of compassion and wisdom, and she is extremely bright with both book knowledge and street savvy. She is proper and particular, graceful, and yet extremely modest. She has her quirks, as we all do, but those only make her more endearing. One of the things that I admire most about her is her uncanny ability to recall dates, times, and events. Her memory is equal to that of a database mainframe. I am in total awe of that. Her sensitivity is unequaled by anyone else I know. Her dedication to her family and friends is unshakable, and she cares deeply for all those she befriends. She can be trusted, and she never breaks a confidence. We had shared many laughs together and grieved together. She is not predictable, but you can count on her stability and level head. She is a gem among women.

Next is Vanessa. She is the one I most connect with. We relate the best. She is the female me and I am the male her. I often jest about us being twins and her being my evil twin. She wasn't happy about that at first, until she realized it was a term of endearment. She is the most special to me.

Vanessa is a free-spirited woman. Highly emotional and high strung, she is thin and fragile in stature, stylish, and flamboyant. Strikingly attractive, she is the firecracker of the group and very intelligent. Vanessa is never short on energy. If you were to observe her from the end of the hallway at work, the image of a hummingbird buzzing from flower to flower would come to mind. She is always on a mission; it is part of her job description and her makeup. She is passionate about her beliefs and viewpoints. She is the one who looks at everything with emotion first and then sorts it out by facts. She has the ability to balance both.

She is married to a wonderful man who worships her. She wants for nothing, and he treats her like a queen. I have to remind her on occasion that "Queen" is my title. For everything she has in her life and lifestyle, she is not pretentious. She loves life and cares deeply for those who are in her inner circle. Everyone should have a Vanessa enriching their life.

Katie, or KT, is the most grounded of the group. She is practical and methodical in her approach to life, family, and friends. She has more love and caring in her than that possessed by the entire population of the city combined. She is married and is the equivalent of a soccer mom to three beautiful children. She is a master of time management, often juggling swimming, flying lessons, volunteer work, and other school activities. She is devoted to her family and the animal rescue mission. I often wonder how she does it all.

KT always seems to be the voice of reason for me. You can count on her to deliver a no-nonsense response to whatever she is approached with. Her ability to process and filter the unnecessary garble out of any situation is uncanny.

Her natural appearance and attention to grooming only add to her physical appeal. She is always totally put together. She is fashionable and trendy at times, but truth be told, she is much more comfortable in jeans and one of her husband's work shirts. Her youthfulness is directly connected to being so active with her children and involved with what they are doing.

The three of them are a major part of and influence in my life. I can't imagine them not being part of it. There are no ego trips; we are all equal in the friendship we share. One of the most amazing qualities of that friendship is that if one of us is going through something, we are all going through it. I am very fortunate and blessed to have them in my life.

We gathered unplanned in Gwen's office, which is the norm for us. It was a daily routine, a ritual. It could happen at any time during the day—it was never scheduled. One of the four of us would just happen into another person's office, and the next thing you know, all four of us were together.

Vanessa, who usually had something to say, started first. One by one, we all became involved in the conversation. We all got our two cents' worth of comments or advice in. Soon, there were several open topics on the table. We always managed to fit our conversations into the day and still get all our work done.

When it was my turn to interject my plans for the weekend with Peter or any new events, I did so. I gave a condensed version of what happened the night before. I recapped the conversation and told them he spent the night. All three were silent and glued to their chairs. They said and asked little until I was finished with my stories. As usual, Vanessa was the first to jump in.

"You got naked?" It seemed that is all she heard—she zeroed in on how we slept, not giving any thought to the rest of what I said. "What about the six-and-two rule? What did you tell him? You are moving, RIGHT?" she insisted. All of it was delivered in her usual high-octane manner.

"Honey, nothing happened and slow down. We didn't do the dirty and we've been naked twice already—on the sailboat outing and the first time he spent the night. I don't see myself moving to Austin, going back to flying and commuting to Houston or Chicago," I said.

"BUT! He's the one. I know it. You know it. HELL! We all know it," she said, getting more animated.

"It's too soon to know anything," I said, trying to be the voice of reason—not my usual role.

After I reeled Vanessa in, she spent the next few minutes verifying the major points of my story. She was trying to put everything in perspective. I could tell she was going into balancing mode. Gwen was the next to comment.

"Well, from what you have said, it sounds like he knows where the relationship is going or where he wants it to go," she said.

"It does sound that way, and yet he is being a little reserved about it as well," I replied.

"But you said the 'L' word was mentioned! That should count for something," Gwen insisted.

"I am not exactly sure in what context that was said. I believe he was sincere. I was when I responded to him saying it, but I'm just not sure," I said.

"That is just you being insecure about everything with the recent events," KT added.

"Possibly. Probably," I conceded.

"Well, all I know is, he is good to you and for you. He has made you happier than you have been in a long time. For that, I am going to send him a Hallmark," Gwen said in her motherly way.

We were interrupted, and our visit was cut short. We split up and went to our offices to start getting some work done. I knew that it was not the last I would hear from them. I was sure I would get a visit from each of them separately sometime throughout the day. They did not disappoint.

Vanessa was the first to make an appearance. I got up from my desk, shut the door, and told her to get it off her chest before she had a stroke. She made a case for keeping an open mind and seeing where it was all leading. She thought the commuting thing was not out of the question. Her delivery was a bit theatrical and slightly dramatic, but there was a lot of merit in what she said. She even left the room and came back with another thought. It all came from a genuine place—her heart—and I loved her for it.

She was followed by KT.

"Hey, what's on your mind?" I asked, setting my work aside.

"You know, this is actually none of our—my—business, except you made it our business when you included us this morning," she began.

"Ouch. Sorry. It was not my intention for you to take this on," I said.

"Too late," she responded.

"Well, it is a catch twenty-two for me. Leave the three of you out of the loop and hear about it later and forever, or tell you about it now and have you all concerned," I explained.

"Difficult decision, but we are concerned for you. You know that what is happening to one is happening to all four," she said.

"I know, and that is why it is all right for you to tell me what is on your mind," I replied.

"Ultimately, the decision is yours, not his or ours to make for you. It is a difficult position to be in. We can only be there for you when he leaves, if he does, or sit here and cry when you say good-bye to us," she said.

"Let's not get ahead of ourselves here. He hasn't even signed anything yet. I appreciate your concern. He isn't even sure what he wants to do yet," I explained.

"I have a feeling that this isn't going to have a good outcome. Nope, nothing good is going to come from this," she said with conviction. "I just have a bad feeling about this all. I can't explain it. There is a dark ending to this."

"KT, it is unlike you to be so negative," I said.

"I'm sorry. Not my intention. I am having a hard time with this. I can't quite wrap my gray matter around it. There is just something uncomfortable about all this," she continued.

"It is all a bit unsettling," I admitted.

"I guess my main concern is that I just don't want you to get hurt by all this. I worry that you are the one who is going to be left standing alone when it is all said and done. Please be careful and think everything through," she said with compassion.

"I will. You know me; I analyze everything to death all the time," I said.

KT got up to leave my office. She made it to the door and I stopped her, saying, "Peter and I have called a truce on talking about it this weekend. He is getting with his lawyer and business manager. He will know more next week from Austin. The main thing is that I am not to be a factor in the decision. I can't be. I don't want that responsibility."

"According to him, you are a factor. Can't see how you're not. It is difficult but manageable," she said, then smiled and walked out.

The conversation between us was upsetting. I had never seen her like that before. I knew she was coming from a place of concern, but I didn't fully understand why she said the things she did. She seemed to have a sixth sense at times, and it was almost as if she could see into the future. I was a witness to it, and she and I both believed in it.

Gwen was the one who spent only a moment in my office. She just confirmed that the three of them were in my corner and would be there when I needed them to be. I think I appreciated that the most.

It was not my intention to get the girls upset, though they seemed to be. We come to each other for support and brainstorm events that are happening in our lives. I have never been a drama queen, and I wasn't going to become one over this. I wanted their feedback on what was going on. Maybe just the fact that it happened out of the blue caused these reactions in them and me. All the unknowns didn't help, either.

I didn't bring a bag with me to work, so I needed to get home, pack some stuff for the weekend, and take a quick shower. My thoughts consumed me on the train ride home—in fact, I was so lost in thought that I almost missed my transfer point. What was I going to do? The girls' options were very workable and not far-fetched at all. Peter's solutions were almost parallel with theirs.

I was in a quandary of my own. I was falling in love, or maybe I was already in love with him, and there was a good possibility that he was moving away. I kept going back to the fact that we hadn't known each other that long and yet we seemed to know each other quite well.

It was a bit too soon to worry about all this—no arguing that. There was a connection between us which was undisputable. There was something so real about how and why it all happened the way it did. It was another life lesson, perhaps.

My life has been barren and void of love and caring. I was at the brink of throwing in the towel on emotional happiness. I was in dating hell, and it seemed as though I could only meet pond scum types. They were emotionally detached, substance-dependent, or married—married to a woman or committed to another man and wanting to step out of their relationship. At my age, it wasn't supposed to be this difficult.

Not being the most put-together kind of guy, I was still ahead of the many I met and dated. Men my age are supposed to have it together, know who they are, to have learned from the past, to be comfortable with it and comfortable with what may happen in the future. This had not been my experience so far.

Then Peter pedaled into my world. He was handsome, secure, and considerate. Polite, not overly ambitious, and yet self-motivated and driven. Caring, compassionate, and full of life. He was my idea of perfection in a man. It was all built into a six foot four frame of modesty and humility.

I called him as I walked home from the train. I gave him my plan and rough time frame. Once inside the condo, my plan fell into place and I was on schedule. Then the phone rang.

"Hey, what's up, honey?" I said.

"I am worried about you. You are taking this a bit casually. You're in turmoil, and given what your dating life has been I am thinking you are going to just throw all this with Peter away and walk away from it." This was KT's opening statement.

"Wow!" I tried to speak and was shut down.

"Just listen for a second. You have been happier than you have been in months, maybe a year or two. He is everything you have ever wanted, talked about having, and dreamed about. Life presents challenges and hurdles. Work this out. It can be done. I know that. Peter knows it is workable and so do you. Don't say or do anything until you have thought it out. You know you have a tendency to speak and act before thinking. DON'T do that this time. You both have called a conversation truce this weekend, and that is a good thing, but you need this and you deserve this and you should have this," she said.

I got my chance to speak. "I'm not blowing anything off. I am not discounting anything. There is a lot to consider here. Nothing is or has been decided. We will just have to wait and see how it all plays out. If this thing between Peter and me had a life span of more than a year, we wouldn't be having this discussion and it wouldn't be an issue for us. Peter has to make all the decisions—he either accepts the proposal or he doesn't. What has you so concerned?" I asked.

"We don't know him. We only know what you have told us. We see what he has done for you and how he makes you feel. I—we—don't want to see you get hurt. That is the bottom line. He goes and you don't—you hurt. You go with him—you hurt in a different way, having to leave friends and family behind," she said.

"Always the mother. You are caring for a husband, three great kids, and that menagerie and you still have room for one more. You are incredible. This really has you bugged. You are feeling or seeing something I'm not. How can I make you feel better about all this? I don't want you so worked up. You know I won't do anything without a consultation session with the three of you. I am not going to do anything silly," I reassured her.

"Well, on one hand, I see that this relationship is a good thing for you, and yet I can't shake a very disturbing feeling that there is something very wrong or that something awful is going to happen. I don't mean to be so amped out over it all. It is just that I sat there this morning and I got a cold chill and was overcome with a feeling of desperation and pain," she said, with sadness in her voice.

"I am not being desperate. I am not desperate to make a decision here, and the decision is not mine to make. Once he makes one, then it will be my time to decide which direction I am going to go. That is where I am with it all. Please be comfortable with that and know that is honestly how I feel," I said.

She didn't comment and changed direction. "What time is he picking you up?"

"He isn't. I am training it up there and I have to run," I answered.

"Have a good time, baby. We will talk later. Bye," she said.

"Bye," I responded.

I blew through the condo and grabbed everything I was taking with me. I called Peter from the train platform and confirmed our plan for when I arrived at our rendezvous spot. I hung up with him and called KT.

When she answered the phone, I told her I loved her for her concern and compassion. I assured her again that nothing was or would be decided until I got all the facts and details. We talked a little longer as the train traveled north. When I got to my stop, I ended the conversation with her and called Peter.

I exited the train station and waited a couple of minutes at the spot where he told me to wait. The car pulled up, and he was smiling that breathtaking smile. He lowered the passenger side window as the car came to a stop.

"Hey, mister. How was your day? Looking for a date?" I joked and returned his smile.

"Yeah, I am looking for a date. How much is one with you going to cost me? Ummm, on second thought, I can't. I am meeting someone kinda special. Maybe another time," he joked back.

"All right, then. It's your loss. I guess I will take the next train back to the city. Besides, you suburb guys are kind of strange," I said, then turned and started to walk away.

"GET IN HERE! I've been waiting all day to see you!" he said.

"It's good to be seen," I quipped, then opened the door and got in.

"We have to make a stop along the way. I also wanted to show you a couple of things," he said.

"Personal guided tour. Cool! Let's go," I replied.

We drove out of the parking lot and were on our way. He pointed out landmarks and other points of interest, all of which were connected to him in some way. I was totally lost—I had no idea where we were.

We stopped at the entrance gate of Northwestern University, where he went to school. The part of campus I was seeing was beautiful. I couldn't believe how pretty it was. He said he would show me around it sometime. We had lunch on part of the north campus, but I didn't get to see the main campus.

He drove and pointed out this and that. All were points of interest in his life, with stories behind them. Each was a piece of who he was and helped formulate the man he had become.

We stopped in front of a building. He told me it was his office and where he lived, just in case I didn't remember. I remembered his mention of the three-story building. I started to get out, thinking that we were at our destination. We weren't.

As I got back into the car, he told me the tour wasn't over and said he had a special surprise waiting for me. He also explained that we needed to make that stop he told me about earlier. I thought back to our conversation earlier that day and couldn't come up with anything that might give me a clue as to where we were going.

Having only been up in that part of the city twice before, I had no idea where we were. I sat back and enjoyed the scenery, conversation, and looking at my chauffeur. We stopped in front of another three-story walk-up building. He flipped open his phone and punched in the number.

"Uh-huh. Out front," he said.

Moments later, the front door opened and a beautiful young woman appeared and started walking towards the car. She beamed with a radiant smile, her long, dark, flowing hair bouncing as she walked our way. She was fashionably dressed and percolated with energy. As she neared the car, I saw the family resemblance. It was a sister—I knew that much.

"Gabby or Dianna?" I asked.

"Gabby," he said.

At that point, he leaned into me and directed his attention to her. He instructed her to hop into the backseat. The door flung open and she came bounding in, the whole time scolding Peter about being late and making us late for dinner.

When there was a break from the verbal judo, I introduced myself. Gabby and I hit it off right away. I found her delightful and refreshing. She was articulate, with a touch of sarcasm, a quality I found fun and liked in people. She continued to razz her brother about being late, while also talking with me.

Peter told me that her nickname was not only short for Gabriella, but for her ability to talk continually and her inability to keep a secret. It was apparent in a matter of minutes.

She very innocently spilled Peter's intentions of having me spend the weekend and said there was a special surprise for me, a romantic brunch on Sunday. She went on to tell me that everyone was waiting at his parents' house and anxious to meet me. That tidbit of information sent me into a tailspin.

Peter quickly interjected that he didn't tell me earlier because he didn't want me to fret about meeting everyone—probably a good idea on his part. He also said he wanted it to be a surprise. It was. He went on to explain that the Sunday brunch thing just slipped out while talking with her. He hoped that I wasn't too upset. I wasn't.

"Honest, it just slipped out this morning when I talked with her, and when Miss Tell-Everyone-in-the-Free-World there got a hold of it, she called my mother. Mom called me immediately and said saying no was not an option. I promised you a great Italian meal, and there is no better place than where we are going," he said.

"Well, this should be interesting. I'm a bit scaly still and not really prepared for a parental meeting, but what the heck," I said.

"They are great people and you will enjoy yourself. They are going to love you," he reassured me.

Gabby piped up from the backseat and informed us that Dianna and her husband Anthony were coming, too, along with Bill and Caroline, Bill being Peter's best friend and Caroline being his wife. She also told us that we didn't hear any of this from her. We all got a chuckle out of that.

Peter and I exchanged glances and I just started to laugh. Gabby was living up to her nickname.

"True to form?" I asked.

"Yep, true to form," Peter replied as we pulled into his parent's driveway.

I was a bit nervous all of a sudden, as I stepped out of the car. Meeting his entire family and family friends! I wasn't prepared. My stomach was feeling a little sour and tied up in small knots. I wasn't quite sure why—I was guessing it was just the insecurities of first-time meetings. These were people that he cared a lot about and were important to him. But how bad could it be? I was sure it was going to be a good evening.

From the moment I entered the house, I was made to feel at home and part of the family. His parents were exceptional people. You could tell they loved their family, both the immediate and extended members. Bill and Caroline arrived with his parents, and Dianna and Anthony arrived shortly after them.

The house was filled with the wonderful aromas of dinner. Everyone was pitching in, helping his mother to prepare the dining room table and finish up the last-minute cooking duties. I offered to help and was turned away, as I was company that night.

I watched as the well-orchestrated event unfolded. They were no strangers to this dinner routine. The spacious dining room amply supported the enormous table that was rapidly filled with silverware, plates, and food. It looked like it was going to be a feast.

It was a typical Italian affair, or at least the kind that I envisioned. A bit stereotypical of me to think, but when I thought about an Italian family gathering, I imagined exactly what I was engaged in. After the dinner prayer, it seemed as though everyone had a platter or serving bowl in his or her hand. They were not only scooping up heaping portions of the feast for themselves, but for one another. There was a lot of activity around the table at first, with serving dishes and platters being passed in all directions. Once everyone was served and had some of everything on his plate, the only task left was to enjoy the delicious meal and savor the good company.

Over dinner, there was an endless stream of conversation, questions for me, and stories about Peter. There was a continuous assortment of hugs, kisses, and love taps, as people were up and down and in and out of their chairs, filling and refilling their plates.

Peter whispered an apology for the questions and promised it would be over soon. I assured him that I didn't mind it at all. If I wanted to dodge any question, I would just ask about something in Peter's childhood and the focus would immediately shift.

The conversation never had a lull in it. At times, it seemed that everyone was talking at once. I lost track of conversations and stories, just because one led into another and that spurred a tangent into another related story. Every once in a while there was a reassuring grip or nudge of my thigh from Peter. He seemed pretty comfortable with me being there, and it appeared as though his family and friends were as well.

There were numerous questions for me. I didn't feel that they were intruding on my privacy, or that I was the star witness in some high-profile court case. They simply expressed total interest in where I grew up and how

I felt about current events. They were fascinated with the fact that I had moved around so much with my career and company. They wanted to hear all about it. It was nice of them to make me feel so at home and not like an outsider.

They were especially comfortable with Peter's lifestyle and mine. No one seemed to be uncomfortable with the fact that I was Peter's date. They all knew who I was to Peter and knew that we were dating. No one put us on the spot, although Dianna did ask me how we met. I told them how our first encounter unfolded—the *Reader's Digest* version.

"That is a cute story—almost a fairy-tale beginning," Dianna said very sincerely.

"Fairy! Who are you calling a fairy?" Peter responded, with a huge grin on his face.

"Oh my God, Jeff, I didn't... I mean ....did I? I wasn't calling you a..." Dianna was a bit flustered.

I stopped her instantly. "I took absolutely no offense. It was kind of a storybook beginning." I didn't want her to be upset.

"It was pretty sweet, actually," Peter said, giving my leg a squeeze.

Dinner was done before I knew it, and I was stuffed. My plate was never allowed to be empty. There was always another scoop of this or that added. It was all so wonderful, I felt compelled to eat it all. With a full belly, great conversation, and lovely company, I had a pleasing feeling of contentment.

The evening then moved into the living room, but only after we all pitched in and helped clean everything up. We all carried something into the kitchen and helped put leftovers in dishes and load the dishwasher, which Gabby volunteered herself and me for. When the chores were done, we settled into the living room and had coffee and dessert. I declined dessert, as I just couldn't eat another bite.

The evening was coming to an end. His friends and family were wonderful people and I really enjoyed meeting them. At the door, his father shook my hand and then wrapped me in a big hug, telling me not to be a stranger and saying I was welcome back anytime—Peter's boyfriend, he said, was always welcome in their home. I thanked him and accepted the open invitation. The boyfriend comment took me aback a little. They considered me his boyfriend? What had he told them? At any rate, it was very nice of them to extend the invitation for future visits.

His mother was also very gracious in her good-byes and with the invite to return anytime. Hugs and kisses were in order. She held me tight and whispered in my ear her desire for Peter and me to continue to see each other. "He's my boy, I love him, and he needs someone like you. I know these things—I'm a mother." Cammy—short for Camellia—was sincere in what she said. I heard it in her voice.

Peter was busy saying his farewells to everyone. The departure at and through the door took about twenty minutes. There was again and again one more thing to say or another hug and kiss to be given. I thanked them again for a wonderful evening, fabulous meal, and exceptional company, and then made my way out the door. With a final wave good-bye, Peter grabbed my hand and we walked down the sidewalk to the car.

Peter pulled into the train station. I was filled with confusion, and it was written all over my face. I heard the door locks click open. He sat there stone faced and serious. I wasn't sure what to do or say. Up to this point, he had not said anything that would make me think that the plans for the weekend had changed. As the car came to a stop, I looked at him inquisitively. I felt panicked.

"Are we going somewhere? Have the plans changed?" I asked timidly.

"Nope," he answered. "Not as far as I am concerned."

"Then what is this all about?" I asked.

"I have something that I want to tell you, and I thought it best to tell you here, where you have the chance to get on a train and run back to the city and not look back," he said.

"All right. Tell me what is on your mind," I said.

"I'm not exactly sure how to tell you this, but here goes. Simply, my family comes with me, Jeffrey, and I want you to come with me as well. I think—no, I know that I don't want to date anyone else. I want it to be just you and me," he said.

"OK, I think that is a good idea. What does the family have to do with it?" I asked.

"I have been placed into a position, in the past, to make a choice between them and someone I dated. I don't want to be in that position again. Now that you have spent the evening with them and have an idea of what they are like, if you don't think you can handle being part of all that commotion—and chaos at times—I am giving you an out," he said.

"An out is not necessary. I think I am good with the family thing. If that is the worst thing that comes with you, then I am feeling pretty lucky," I said.

"That makes me feel better," he responded. "I am glad that you feel that way. I know that I threw you into that mix unexpectedly this evening. Sorry about that, but honestly it just happened and sort of got out of my control."

"The family thing didn't really concern me, but don't you think this was a bit dramatic, the train station and all?" I said to him with a smile, smacking him in the arm.

"Yeah, I guess it was. You should have seen your face…priceless," he joked back. "I won't do that again."

"Damn straight you won't!" I said. "The line has been drawn in the sand, mister. I may not get even for this right away, but don't ever turn your back on me."

"Sounds fair," he said as he leaned in and kissed me.

"Can we please get out of here? I can't say hanging out at a train station is my idea of having a great time," I said.

He put the car into drive, and off to his place we went. We were there in a matter of minutes. When we got up to his condo, he wanted to give me the tour. I was looking forward to seeing where and how he lived. I was sure it would be a reflection of the man.

It was a spacious and sleek space. Everything about it was totally him, as I suspected. Everything pleasantly reeked of his personality and who he was. It was laid out and decorated as I envisioned it would be.

It was well decorated, modern in design, and comfortable. The tour included anecdotes about different artifacts that were placed around on shelves and tables. He was extremely proud of his home, though not in a pretentious way—he was very modest about it all.

The tour ended in a comfortable den upstairs on what was the third floor. He dimmed the lights and lit a few candles. He hit the power button on the stereo, and the house filled with music. He left me there and went to get champagne from downstairs.

When he returned, I was seated on the love seat absorbed in the music and the atmosphere he had created. He joined me there, and I turned to face him. He reached over, placed an arm around my shoulder, and nestled me closer. We sat silently.

Time passed slowly. We sat there and enjoyed each other's company. I broke the embrace, stood, and extended my hand. He looked up and gave me his, and I gave it a tug and pulled him to his feet. We stood there embraced in each other's arms, swaying back and forth. We started to slow dance in the middle of the room. It was as if the music was doing a slow seduction on us. We were immersed in the moment. Nothing else was a concern—it was just us.

His face was buried in the crook of my neck. I could feel his breath against my skin, and an occasional brush of his lips and quick dart of the tip of his tongue. It sent shivers up and down my spine. I felt so alive and safe with him. It was ecstasy, without the act of physical relations—our shared sensuality.

He took my hand and led me to his bedroom. We lay down, facing each other. The soft glow of the street lamp light caressed us. Elton John played in the background. He was singing, "Something about the way you look tonight." It was the right song for the moment.

With our clothing removed, we softly stroked and caressed each other. There was no urgency to the passion and sensuality. There was an intimacy of the touch that was being explored and enjoyed. We were not there to consummate our relationship—it was about the pure enjoyment of being there together.

I rolled him onto his back and kissed him. He placed his arms up over his head and locked his fingers together, resting his head in his palms. He closed his eyes tightly as my fingertips slid up and down his chest and abdomen. He appeared to be totally relaxed and almost in a trancelike state.

I stopped abruptly. "Peter," I whispered, "we have to stop this. I hope you don't mind and will understand."

"I know, baby. It's that six-and-two rule. I was really enjoying that. Do we have to stop?" he asked.

"Actually, no, that is not it. I am thinking that the candles in the other room are going crazy. Look at the reflection in the window," I replied.

"OH, HELL! I forgot about them!" he shouted. He rolled out of bed and hurried down the hall. As he reached the other room, he yelled, "Jeff, call nine-one-one! Get the fire department."

I sprang out of bed and ran down the hall, yelling, "Where is your phone? Is there one in the bedroom? Hell, I will get mine out of my bag."

I grabbed my cell phone out of my bag and my underwear off the floor, and back down the hall I went. I continued down the hall, thinking he didn't hear me. I was trying to power up the cell and get my foot into my underwear at the same time. I was hopping about, trying to keep my balance and talk to him all at once. I had my foot caught in the leg opening, hopping up and down, and was pulling on the waistband to get them on—then I heard the snickers.

"I'm sorry, Jeff. I just couldn't resist. Don't be mad." he said, trying to suppress his laughter. "I'm not sure why it looked out of control. Everything is fine. All the candles are blown out now."

I just pointed a finger at him. "I will get you. I will SSSOOOOO get you!" I warned.

"Come on, let's go back to bed," he said, and then busted into laughter.

He grabbed my hand, I let go of my waistband, and my underwear fell to the floor. I bent down, grabbed them, and threw them at him. I walked back and sat up against the headboard. He returned with our glasses of champagne, handed me the glasses, lay down, and put his head in my lap. We were soon in a prone position together and facing the same way. His back was against me, and my arms encircled him. We closed the distance between us and fell asleep.

CHAPTER 6

Favorable Impressions

In the morning, we lay in bed without any need to get up and get moving. Gabby called twice that morning. He let the answering machine pick up the first call, and after she started talking on the second, he answered it.

I showered as he called his sister back. There was a cup of coffee on the vanity for me. When I returned to the bedroom, I noticed something that I hadn't the night before—a set of French doors. The doors were open and led to a private balcony patio area. He called for me from there. The brightness of the morning sun assaulted me as I stepped through the threshold and onto the patio. This area offered seclusion from his neighbors, without creating a feeling of encapsulation. He sat in the morning sunlight having his coffee as I joined him in his private sanctuary.

"Hey, you don't look like you are peeling as badly. It may even be turning color," he remarked.

"I think the peeling stage is over," I agreed.

"Hang out here while I take a shower," he suggested.

The sun was warm, but you could tell it was soon going to be fall. Peter returned from his shower with a fresh carafe of coffee. We sat and discussed the plans for the day. A bike ride through the campus, the exhibit at the art museum, and lunch with Gabby were all on the table.

I suggested that we call Gabby and have her join us for the day. This seemed to please him, as he was especially close to her. She may not have the ability to keep things private. She saw nothing wrong with the "sharing of information," as she called it, but she was a wonderful person. I considered it a special talent of hers. She was who she was and she considered her life an open book, so why not everyone else's? She was totally refreshing and free spirited.

The phone rang as we finished up our coffee. It was his sister. She gladly accepted our invitation and said she would be over in an hour. Bill called next and invited Peter and me to have a late dinner on the boat. He asked if that might be all right with me, and I accepted without hesitation. I loved being out on the boat and water.

The day was arranged. We would get me home for different clothes and my bike and pick up Gabby along the way. Dinner wouldn't be until 8:00 that evening. We decided to bike to the museum and then work our way back to my place. We wouldn't be able to bike the campus, but that was all right—there would be other opportunities for that.

His sister was a wealth of knowledge about the exhibit we went to see and full of a variety of fun facts about the city. We were almost ignoring Peter as we biked and walked through the exhibit. I apologized for that and he dismissed it, saying that he was enjoying watching the two of us get to know each other better.

We were back at the condo before I knew it. It seemed as though the day had gone by so quickly. I packed some clothes and other necessities. We packed up the car, and we were on our way north to his house. When we arrived, the three of us shared coffee and some conversation on his patio deck. It had been a great day, and dinner on the boat was going to finish it off nicely. After Gabby left, we finished our coffee out on the deck before showering and getting ready for dinner with Bill and Caroline.

"I am so happy you like Gabby. Jason didn't like her at all. He thought she talked too much and was silly and a nuisance. They didn't get along at all, as much as Gabby tried," he said.

"I like being around her. She is full of life and extremely likable. She is intelligent and free spirited. She is adorable. Jason? An ex?" I asked.

"Yeah, it ended three years ago. He didn't like my family, especially Gabby. My family tried to get along with him, but he just didn't want that. Mom never warmed up to him. When he was with me, they were all very hospitable to him, but truth be told, I think it was only because I was dating him," he explained.

"That is too bad. They are nice people. I can't imagine anyone not liking them," I said.

"They took to you last night, I could tell. I knew they would. I was pretty happy to see it all unfold," he said.

"Good thing, huh? Always makes it easier with the parents. Speaking of parents, I hadn't the chance to tell you that my mother and sister are coming in next weekend. If time permits, I would like for you to meet them and for them to meet you," I said.

"Oh, no, I have to do the family thing?" he said with a grin.

"Fair is fair, mister," I replied. "At least you have a little advance notice."

"…to sweat about it," he commented.

"You have nothing to worry about. Don't plan anything for next Saturday," I said.

"Saturday it is. Any plans on what we might be doing?" he asked.

"None. We will just play it by ear," I said.

The phone rang and ended our conversation. It was Gabby. She actually wanted to talk with me. Peter gave me the phone. While I was talking with her, he became animated and motioned that he was going to take a shower. I motioned back OK, and off he went. After a few minutes of talking with her, I told her I needed to take a shower and get ready for dinner. I didn't want to be the one that would make us late. She told me that I was going to have a good time and said Bill and Caroline were great people and good friends. We said our good-byes, and I hung up.

I headed downstairs on a little side trip before stripping off my clothing and entering the bathroom. I found the largest tumbler glass I could and filled it with the chilled water from the refrigerator. It was payback time for the train station and candle pranks.

I entered the bathroom in stealth mode. His back was towards me as I snuck into the room. The CD player was blasting out Elton John, and I was confident that he didn't hear me enter or know that I was there. I reached the shower and gave it a tug. The metal strip and magnet made a snap-click noise, and I readied myself for a quick attack. He was shampooing, and his back was to me, so I didn't think he had heard the click.

"Are you going to join me? What a nice surprise," he said, without turning to me.

"I thought I would surprise you," I said.

With that said, the door swung open and the water went sailing. He turned right at that time and caught most of it on his chest and abs. He let out a scream that was worthy of some B-rated slasher movie. There was a little water left in the bottom of the glass, and I finished by pouring it down his back.

"Hey, what gives?" he said.

"That was the first payback for the pranks from yesterday," I explained.

"Fuck, that was cold! And so was the water," he said, laughing.

I started laughing with him. The look on his face was priceless. I entered the shower, and he washed my back. We finished the shower, dried off, and dressed. We weren't expected at dinner for another forty-five minutes. We spent the time talking—our conversation went back to the one we had left unfinished earlier.

He told me that he was feeling scared about entering a relationship because of the past one with Jason and with the pending business deal. He also said that he had spent some time thinking about us. He wasn't sure what was going to happen professionally, but felt so comfortable about him and me that he didn't want to risk losing me.

He was thinking about a future for us. I sat there listening as he went on to tell me that he hadn't felt this way about anyone before, including Jason. He knew that it was unfair for him to ask me to enter into a relationship with him, with all that was going on, but felt confident it would all work out.

I had been thinking about us as well. We had only had stolen moments, up to this point, to talk about it all. It was something that we were going to have to dedicate some time to. I agreed there was a lot to discuss, and we called a truce for the weekend—a good idea, I thought. We would have the time to talk, and there were things that I wanted to tell him as well. I assured him that we were on a level playing field with what we felt and thought. I did add that I knew how I felt and I was feeling comfortable with the decisions that I had made so far, where it concerned him and me and the future. He looked at me and grinned and simply said, "Sweet."

And yet even with all these realizations, both his and mine, I was still having these unsettling feelings. I couldn't quite put my finger on it, but it was there. A whole gambit of emotions and thoughts were going through my head. What did it all mean?

When we arrived at the harbor, dinner was already being prepared on the grill and things were being stowed on the boat for our dinner cruise. Once dinner was prepared, we all helped cast off from the slip, and out onto the lake we went.

Caroline and Bill were great hosts. They had thought of everything for the evening. Our conversations flowed easily from one topic to another. They were very accepting of Pete and me, and their affection for Peter was obvious.

Caroline and I were involved in a separate conversation from Bill and Peter. She was an interesting woman. I enjoyed listening to her points of view on different current events and topics. She was a lawyer, although she didn't care for the current state of the profession and considered herself a people's lawyer. She liked her small practice and wasn't a corporate ladder climber, as she put it. I found her genuine and sincere.

Peter looked over at me and winked. I smiled in return. He and Bill finished their conversation and dinner preparations and walked our way. Peter sat down between my legs and rested his arms on my knees.

Caroline leaned over to me, pointed to Peter and said, "Jason would never allow that. He thought we were the uptight ones."

"We all have our comfort level—maybe he wasn't comfortable with PDA," I said.

"Yes, we all have our comfort zones. However, we tried to make him feel comfortable, but he just didn't seem to want to accept our hospitality and efforts," Bill added.

"I don't know much about him. It isn't that important to me, though. I have met you both and his family, and I don't see how anyone could be uncomfortable with any of you. I am comfortable and hope that you are all with me," I said with sincerity.

"I am," Peter said.

"To be honest with you, Jeff, I think we all might have been a little nervous at first last night at dinner," Caroline said.

"I know I was. I am not always good with first impressions. I get very shy and reserved, and that is sometimes misinterpreted. I hope that wasn't the case last night. You all made me feel so welcomed. Thanks," I said.

"I didn't get that impression," Bill interjected.

"Good. Thanks for including me this evening. I really enjoy being on the boat and on the water," I said.

"Well, I think it was easy for all of us. I also think we were relieved that it turned out like it did and we didn't have to endure another... how did Peter describe it? Oh, yeah—Pissy Queen. Isn't that what you called him?" asked Caroline.

I just started laughing, as did the other three. Caroline's sincere and innocent delivery made her even more endearing to me. Their openness and honesty throughout the evening only affirmed why Peter held them in such high regard.

I explained to Caroline that I had no intentions of becoming a "Pissy Queen." I found that behavior totally unnecessary and oftentimes offensive. I jokingly gave them permission to shoot me if I ever started going down that path.

"Don't get us wrong, Jeff," Bill interjected. "We liked Jason, we wanted to include him, and Peter's family wanted to include him as well. He just didn't want to be included. I got the impression he didn't want to share Peter's time."

"I don't want to talk about him in front of Jeff. I think that is unfair, but...he was welcomed by everyone and he just wasn't interested in being part of it," Peter said softly.

"His loss, then. Sometimes people put up barriers and they are hard to break down. I'm sure he was a nice guy. You all made the effort and the rest was up to him," I added.

Something in the conversation led us to another topic, and nothing else was said about Jason. Dinner was set up and we prepared our plates and settled into the task at hand—eating. We were all hungry. Peter and Bill took turns sailing us around in the open waters of Lake Michigan. We sailed out far enough to get a great view of the shoreline. Looking south, the city was preparing to greet the evening as night fell. The skyscrapers and other buildings that formed the shoreline were visible. One by one and floor by floor, each building that dotted the shoreline became illuminated.

The evening ended about midnight, and Peter and I said our good-byes. Our hosts were spending the night on the boat. In the car on the way to Peter's, he apologized for the conversation about Jason. No apology was needed, and I told him so. It was part of his past. He explained that everyone was anxious to meet me, as Jason was the first "boyfriend" that he took home, their only point of reference.

We really hadn't talked about our past relationships prior to this. It just didn't seem necessary or important. He went on to tell me that he didn't take anyone he dated home to meet family and friends. When I asked him why, he explained that they were short term and it was a personal decision to only introduce his family and friends to someone he was serious about.

I told him I was comfortable with everyone that I had met so far and that I looked forward to seeing and spending time with all of them again. I didn't elaborate on the topic much and finished that it was important to me that they all liked me because it would be easier for him and me both. We changed the topic as we drove back to his place.

Neither Peter nor I slept in late, as a rule. Sunday morning we remained in bed until about 8:00. We were awake earlier, but just lounged around in bed for a while. He got out of bed once to get coffee for us. It just felt so right to be so close to him. I kept thinking about how lucky I was.

Peter got up first, showered, and prepared our Sunday brunch as I showered. I found him in the kitchen, just finishing the packing of the brunch basket. We dressed and grabbed everything, and off we went. We were going to go to one of his favorite spots along the lakeshore.

When we arrived, it was evident why this spot was his favorite. It was lush with trees, and seasonal flowers were blooming. The trees offered a shaded canopy for us, and we had a panoramic view of the lake. The grassy area was well trimmed and offered the perfect spot to spread out the blanket and brunch.

I just kept looking at him as he busied himself setting things up. Every time I looked at him, I felt my feelings for him grow deeper and stronger. I need to disclose something that I was holding back from him. I felt it was time to share it with him. I hoped it would be received well. I was sure it would be.

We sat there looking out over the water and taking in the splendor of the surroundings. I sat looking at him, as much as—if not more than—at the beauty of his favorite lakefront place. I was absorbed in his radiance. Mother Nature had supplied us with a magnificent day and beautiful backdrop. Abundant sunshine, warm caressing breezes, and a crystal blue cloaked our morning. The sunlight danced off the ripples of the lake. It was as if someone had lit hundreds of thousands of sparklers at one time, as the breezes shimmered across the water.

I decided it was time to tell him. "Peter," I began.

"Yeah," he answered.

"I want and need to tell you something. Don't interrupt because you know how we get off on different conversational tangents at times. I need to tell you something and it might complicate our lives a little. I don't think it will," I said.

"More than they are already with everything that is going on in my life right now?" he asked.

"Don't interrupt," I repeated.

"OK. What is on your mind?" he asked.

As I began to speak, from behind me I heard, "Hey, you guys! I didn't think you two would still be here. Fancy meeting you two here. What a great surprise!"

Peter instantly looked pretty upset. I glanced over at our surprise visitor and back at Peter. I knew, by the look on his face, it was an unwelcome intrusion. I looked at him and smiled, as I shifted around and started to get up.

"Your fault...you told her," I whispered as I got to my feet and turned. "Gabby! How wonderful to see you. Drop the bike and join us. Your brother has prepared a great lakefront brunch."

"Oh, I don't know. Judging from the look on his face, it might not be a good idea. I didn't know you two would actually still be here," she said.

"Nonsense. Stay. Besides, you are already here now, so join us," I said.

"As always, your timing is impeccable or awful—you pick," Peter said, as he stood and gave her a huge brotherly hug and kissed her on the cheek.

Peter looked at me as he hugged her. I could tell from his facial expression and tone of voice that he was not happy to see her. I shrugged, smiled, and winked at him. We would make the best of it. I really didn't mind. Our conversation could wait. There would be another time to tell him what I wanted to say.

Maybe Gabby's interruption was a sign to wait, and I had to admit I was a little relieved. All I really knew at that moment was that she was there and we would enjoy her company. Her brother loved her very much and she was very dear to him, and although he might not be happy with her at this particular moment, it would pass quickly.

We refreshed our mimosas and offered her one, along with a plate of fruit and cheese and assorted other goodies that Peter had packed. In a stolen moment, when Gabby was not within earshot, Peter apologized for the interruption. I told him it was nothing to be concerned about and suggested that we just enjoy ourselves.

"I sure am glad you like her and you aren't upset. She really likes you and she likes to be involved. Jason wasn't as accommodating as you. She is a bit protective of me, and I think in her own innocent way, she doesn't see any harm in including herself. I would have preferred she didn't show up this morning. This was supposed to be just you and I. Thanks for being so kind," he said.

"Don't be silly, and DON'T be hard on her, either. She is wonderful, and I like her a lot. You do, too. That is very evident," I said.

"It leaves little time for us to be alone," he added.

"Shit, man, we have all day—well, most of the day, anyway. It is nothing to worry about," I said.

"Actually, we don't," he said.

"Huh?" I replied.

"There is this family thing today. The annual family and friends barbecue is this afternoon. I thought I told you about it. I didn't? Did I forget to tell you?" he asked.

"That would be NO! And YES, you forgot," I playfully answered. "Well, when we are finished here, you can drop me off at the train. It's been a wonderful morning and great weekend. I have loved every minute of it," I said.

"Aren't you going to be there, Jeff? You are invited—Mom and Dad insist," Gabby said, re-entering the conversation.

"Thanks, Gab, but I think I am going to have to pass. I have to be at work at 5:00 in the morning tomorrow, and I have a volunteer commitment at mass this evening, and…"

"I was counting on you going with me," Peter said, looking a bit hurt.

"I would love to go, but I have a dozen things to do that I didn't get done this weekend. I just can't. I am sorry. It is a little late to get a sub for me at mass this evening. Thanks, but I am going to have to pass, I am afraid," I said.

Peter didn't appear convinced that it was just domestic duties and mass that were keeping me from going. I knew that the subject would be approached again, and it was. Gabby seemed to accept the explanation and backed away from strong-arming me into going.

We spent the balance of our time sharing stories, throwing a fabric Frisbee around, and just enjoying ourselves. Gabby was the first to announce that she needed to leave, as she had promised her parents that she would help set up and prepare. We all took note of the time and packed everything up. Gabby took off on her bike, and Peter and I made our way to his car. It was a good morning. I felt all giddy inside, like a schoolgirl on prom night. This time spent together would be fondly remembered.

"Don't apologize," I said as we backed out, sensing it was coming.

"Well, I was going to. It was to be just you and me. Gabby wasn't included—she was not part of the vision or plan for this morning. It was nice of you to include her, though. She was thrilled," he said.

"I was thrilled you didn't strangle her," I responded.

"It was a fleeting thought, I must admit," he said as his cell phone rang.

I was trying not to pay much attention to his conversation. I was busy taking my final look at where we had spent the morning and early afternoon. I didn't want to appear to be eavesdropping. It did become clear that his answers were short and brief.

Flipping his phone closed, he said, "That must be a world record, even for her."

"Gabby?" I asked.

"Yep, Gabby. That was mom, and she knows that you aren't coming this afternoon. I told her I would explain later," he said.

"Man, she is quick," I commented.

"Yep, she is. She must have had her cell with her and called while biking over there," he said.

"Well, let's go over and I will offer my regrets and explain. We don't want your mom to be upset," offered.

"Once you're in, you may be held captive and not be allowed to escape," he warned.

"I'll risk it. Besides, you would be my captor. I can think of worse fates," I said, raising an eyebrow and giving a grin.

"Hmmm. There is a thought," he said, giving me a devilish grin.

We arrived at his parents' house, and I apologized to his parents. They were more understanding than I was led to believe they would be. Peter dropped me off at the train, and I was on my way home. I was feeling a bit empty. I was realizing how much I really enjoyed spending time with him.

CHAPTER 7

Scoring Big Time

It was after 3:00 in the afternoon when I entered the condo. I was feeling rushed with all I had to get accomplished before my mass commitment. I managed to get everything done and make it to mass on time. It was after 9:00 when I returned home that evening. I showered and began to unwind from the day. I was on the couch, stretched out, reflecting on all the events of an action-packed weekend, when the phone rang.

The phone had rung about twelve times earlier in the day. The calls were from friends and family, who had a variety of excuses and comments as to why they didn't call my cell. I got the ever popular "It's never on" (true), followed by "Thought you might be at work" (for forty-eight hours?), and the all-famous, "Thought you might be out of town" (how would you know unless you called to find out?). The new one that was added was "We thought you might be spending time with Peter and didn't want to disturb you" (very considerate). I was simply amused and thanked them all for their consideration.

This phone call was from Peter. He told me to turn on my computer and then hung up. I did as I was instructed, and discovered an instant message and an invite to view a webcam. I accepted the invitation and settled into my chair. When the picture appeared, it was Peter, Gabby, and their parents.

I typed:

>   *Hey there!*

They responded:

>   *We just wanted to say good night. Hope we didn't wake you.*

I answered:

>   *Nope, just about to head off to bed.*

They replied:

>   *We missed you this evening. Sweet dreams!*

I responded:

>   *How sweet of you all. Thanks! I wish I could have been there.*

Gabby and her parents disappeared from the picture. It was just Peter and I. He left the cam on, but didn't type anything. I saw him dialing his cell phone. My phone rang, and the picture went black.

"Hey, mister," I said, as I answered the phone.

"I just wanted to call and say good night, and the family wanted in on it as well. You were the talk of the evening. I think they like you and you are stuck with them," he said.

"I thought about calling you earlier, but didn't want to interrupt. Have you been having a good time?" I asked.

"You are always thinking about everyone else. I am pretty lucky, I think. Yes, it's always a good time, but I have missed having you here," he said.

"I think I am the lucky one. You have no idea what you have done for me. I will be forever grateful to you," I said.

"Hey, I know we didn't get to finish our conversation this morning. Sorry. Right now might not be a good time, with everyone around…" He stopped talking, as I heard people calling him from the background.

We finished our conversation, though I was unable to assure him that it wasn't anything bad and that it could wait. I could tell by the racket in the background that something was going on and he was missing it. I told him to hang up and said we would talk tomorrow.

We hung up, and I went to bed. It was a GREAT weekend.

The next couple of days at work were hectic and extremely busy. I didn't have much time to do anything but put out fires. Everything that came across my desk was a hot item that needed my immediate attention. I worked a twelve-hour day on Monday and even took work home with me. Tuesday at work wasn't much better, but I wasn't going to be late getting out of there on time. It was bowling night, and I needed the relaxation time. My team was a great group of men and we had a good time together. We were victorious that evening, and the five of us decided to meet at our sponsor's bar for a drink.

As we were packing our stuff up, one of my teammates was making a bunch of noise about some extremely handsome guy standing behind us. His hormones were racing and he said he was in total lust. I didn't pay much attention to his ramblings and finished gathering my stuff. At his insistence, I looked up in the direction he gestured, but I didn't see anyone and couldn't locate the guy he was talking about. When I finished packing my stuff and looked up, I saw him. I suggested a cold shower was in order for my teammate and told him he wasn't going to get the man of his lustful ramblings.

"He wants me, Jeff. I can tell. He is playing it cool, but there is definitely a look of want in his eyes for me," Stephen said with confidence.

"Well, it isn't going to happen!" I said flippantly.

"You never know," he said.

"You're right, you never know, but it isn't going to happen," I quipped.

Stephen expounded upon what he would give or do to have a chance with the guy against the wall. As he continued his rambling, the man started walking towards us. I quickly nudged Stephen to get his attention. Stephen was going on about how he just knew the guy was going to break down and surrender, claiming it was just a matter of time and "wall man" wanted him.

I called Stephen one raging hormone as the handsome wall guy got closer. When he was about three feet away, he pulled out from behind his back three purple irises—my favorite flower.

"Hey, handsome. You need a ride home tonight?" he asked, smiling and handing me the flowers.

"Hey, mister! What a surprise! And yeah, I would love one. I have to console Stephen first and put my stuff away," I said.

"I'll wait for you out front in the car," he said, then winked and walked away.

My team gathered around me, wanting to get the scoop on who that was. I didn't have time and promised that I would fill them in next week. I handed Stephen a napkin to cry in and apologized for messing with him. He only had one thing to say and that was to call me a bitch and a damn lucky one at that.

Once in the car, we determined that we would grab some fast food and head to the lake and eat. It was a cool evening out. It wasn't cold—it was just the first cool evening as the summer was slowly changing into fall. We ate in the car and talked, then grabbed two blankets out of the backseat and went out to sit on the hood and enjoy the evening.

We sat leaning against the windshield, staring up at the stars. The moon was full and radiant. The stars seemed to be brighter and more numerous than on other evenings. We both were lost in our thoughts. I wasn't sure where his thoughts were taking him, but mine were a million light-years away, in a place where we would always be together like this, content in just being in each other's company and an eternity of harmonious bliss. We sat there gazing skyward.

He broke the silence. "I've missed you the past two days."

"I was having Peter withdrawals myself," I responded.

"We both have been extremely busy," he remarked.

"I didn't like it, either. I needed and wanted to see you," I continued.

"I hope you didn't mind me just showing up at bowling," he said.

"Not at all—glad that you did. Are you spending the night?" I asked.

"Can't. Would like to, but I can't. Conference call with the Austin people in the morning and Bill wants a breakfast meeting prior to that. You understand," he said.

"Yep, I do. It is important to have everything in order," I answered. I instantly disliked those Austin people.

"We will be trying to pin them down on a couple of deal breaker items. It will be interesting," he said.

"We might want to think about getting me home then and you on your way home. It is almost 11:00," I said.

"Ten more minutes," he replied.

He was so sweet when he said that. I wanted a lifetime, but would settle for ten more minutes. I felt so secure and happy with him. I had not felt that way in years. I needed to tell him that, but didn't. I didn't want to add to the confusion and conflict he was already experiencing over this pending deal.

He dropped me off and was on his way home. He would get enough sleep this way. It was an important meeting. I went to bed, and I said a silent prayer that it would all work out as it was meant to be. I wanted what was right for him. If he accepted the offer, I had the resources to make things work, in the short term, anyway. I flew for free, and had five weeks of vacation, which could be taken a day at a time for long weekends. I had a flexible work schedule, for the most part, and felt confident we would be able to find something that was workable for both of us.

I couldn't sleep. I got up and sat thinking in one of my big overstuffed chairs. My mind raced with thoughts of him and what was going to happen. I wanted to throw all caution to the wind and move with him, if he accepted the offer. I didn't like the idea of a commuting relationship. There is too much stress involved, too little time, and an unfulfilling feeling about it. I had done that once before and vowed I wouldn't do it again. I realized I might have to re-think that.

I needed to consider why I was opposed to moving as well. I wanted to be close to my family. My mother was alone and had lived alone since my father passed away. That concerned me. I wanted to be close enough to get home, when and if I needed to be. It was the peace of mind I needed, and my mother needed as well. I still considered the fact that I could get home from almost anywhere. Being where I was, was the comfort zone that I was most happy with.

My brain wouldn't shut off. I sat there in my chair, prayer candle lit, smooth jazz playing. I lay across the arms of the chair and stared at the ceiling. What to do? He and I needed some face-to-face time, real time to talk.

The next morning at work I got a call from Peter. The conference call had gone well. He and Bill were pleased. The people in Austin sounded positive and determined to make it happen. It was officially in the works and things were progressing smoothly—as smoothly as business negotiations do.

There were things Peter and Bill needed to do. They would be working late and numerous hours. I needed to prepare for my mother and sister's visit. There would be little time for Peter and me the remainder of the week.

They arrived on Friday morning. We unloaded the car, made some coffee, and caught up on current family events and gossip. I had our days and evenings planned. We were going to be busy this visit. It was important to spend time together, but I also wanted to be the city ambassador this weekend and show them the sights.

At my mother's insistence, we walked the lakefront first; then came the grocery shopping and cooking dinner at my place. Saturday was filled with art exhibits, Sears Tower observation deck, and my mother's favorite, the Lincoln Park Zoo. Saturday also included dinner with Peter, when they met him for the first time. Dinner was flawless. My mother and sister were in love with Peter, and they hit it off perfectly. He was the center of attention and was enjoying every moment of it.

Sunday was loosely planned. We had breakfast at one of my favorite diners and took a sightseeing boat tour. We made a couple of short side trips to see some of the more interesting sights. It seemed that as soon as they got there, they were packing to leave. There was never enough time with these quick, three-day weekend visits.

I spoke with Peter late Sunday night. I found out that he and Bill had completed the mission of gathering documents and papers and getting them arranged for shipping first thing Monday morning. He was relieved that it was all over. Now he would have to sit back and wait for a counteroffer. He was pensive, yet excited about the prospects. His outlook was good. He had to live and work somewhere and he was happy here and probably would be in Austin as well.

Monday afternoon Peter called to say that he and Bill would be flying to Austin on Tuesday. He wasn't sure what all it would entail. He and Bill hadn't had a chance to go over everything, but Bill was going to fill him in that evening. He would most likely be gone for three days. My heart sank as I hung up the phone. I knew it was a finalized deal. I don't know how I knew it—I just knew.

We were beyond the six-and-two rule, which my friends maintained I was silly to have. I maintained that if you allowed physical intimacy to happen too soon, it could cloud your judgment about someone. Physical dates are OK, but if you are serious about a person, or feel there is potential for a long-term relationship, the rule is necessary to keep everything in perspective. It is a check and balance system. Physical attraction is important, even necessary, but when sex happens too soon, it adds a different dimension to the emotional aspect of a relationship.

It was time, however. I was sure I was in love with him. I had every indication of it. I couldn't go any extended period of time without thinking of him. I craved being with him. And most importantly, my heart told me so. I knew before the six-and-two rule was satisfied. Taking the little extra time only fortified that for me.

I spent spare time in my week, while he was gone, planning a special dinner and evening for him. I knew where I wanted to have dinner, I knew how I was going to tell him, and I knew how I wanted the remainder of the evening to go. I thought it through, worked out the details, and then called my friend Greg.

Greg had a flair for these kinds of things; he lived for them. I explained what I was thinking, and he took control of everything. He assured me that he would have it all worked out and we could go over all the details on Thursday or Friday night. I trusted him, and I knew he would do a good job.

Saturday morning, I called Peter and suggested to him what to pack and wear that evening. He was suspicious at first. I wasn't answering any questions. I just suggested he relax and reassured him it was a good thing. I had some preparations for the evening to finish and then all there was to do was to get ready and wait for Peter's arrival and the confirmation call that everything was set.

Peter arrived just as inquisitive as he had been that morning. He accepted that it was a surprise, but still wanted to know what he was in for. He finally surrendered to the fact that I wasn't giving anything up. I was busting at the seams to tell him and couldn't wait until the confirmation call came and we could leave.

The call came in, and I tossed Peter his jacket. I didn't think we would need jackets, but I wanted to have them just in case. We left the condo, and walked across the street and through the tunnel under Lake Shore Drive, heading south along the lake. The sun was lowering behind the buildings to the west. We walked together side by side and talked about whatever interested us, and that kept him from asking where we were going.

I distracted Peter's attention any way I could as we neared our destination. I didn't want him to see it too soon. I had planned and Greg had worked hard on the surprise factor. I pointed out different buildings and asked some pretty stupid questions, just to keep him occupied.

The cloud wisps in the western horizon took on a magnificent orange-red color. They were absorbing the sinking sun's last vibrant light. We watched them as they spread thin and then vanished. When we were close enough, and because I didn't think I could distract him much longer, I lightly took hold of his arm and led him in the right direction. He looked at me as I steered him to the left.

"We have arrived," I announced. "Take a look ahead and to the left."

He followed my pointing finger. "That is for us? You had this arranged for us?" he asked with amazement.

"I did. This is just for you and me," I answered.

"Hey? Isn't this where we met?" he asked.

"Yep, that it is. Come on," I said.

He stood still for a moment, looking at what was awaiting us. I was rather impressed with what Greg had done as well. Greg did a wonderful job. There were about thirty luminary bags placed all around, all white, flickering with candlelight. Music was playing from a sound system that Greg had rigged up. Greg added ferns and potted plants around for a natural touch. Flowing fabric panels were suspended from the tree branches.

In the center of it all was a dining table set for two. It was draped in white linen, which swayed in the light lake breeze. Champagne and wine was chilling, and the grill was set off to the side. Greg was standing at the grill cooking until he heard us, and then he approached the table. He was wearing a white shirt and black pants. He insisted that he serve dinner, even though I told him it wasn't necessary.

Peter and I approached the table. Peter looked a bit awestruck. I had given Greg an idea or two and asked for suggestions and he really put it all together well. I walked alongside Peter, glancing over in his direction to get a read on his thoughts, but couldn't. What might he be thinking? Had I made a mistake?

"Good evening, Gregory," I said playfully, as we walked past him, looking around at all he had created, giving him a thumbs-up and a wink of approval.

"Good evening, gentlemen," he replied.

"Peter, Greg. Greg, Peter." I kept the introduction short.

"Nice to meet you," Peter said softly as he shook Greg's hand. "You did this, set this all up for us?" he asked, smiling at me, but directing his attention to Greg.

"They were all Jeff's ideas. I just helped make them materialize," Greg responded modestly.

As we walked among the luminaries, Greg placed arrangements of fresh and fake flowers. White Christmas lights were hanging from the branches, along with the flowing sheer material that wound around tree trunks. Candle globes were wedged into the tree branches, where they V'ed apart. The table was set as it would be in a five-star restaurant.

Peter reached for my hand and squeezed it tightly. Greg poured a glass of champagne for each of us and suggested that we walk towards the water, while he put the finishing touches to dinner. Glasses in hand, we wandered around looking at everything and then headed towards the very spot where we met.

The evening sky was turning dark. The moon was full and just barely visible at the moment. Stars were just beginning to twinkle. It promised to be a beautiful sight, in the clear, warm Indian summer evening. We sat there holding hands and saying little. We glanced at each other and just smiled. I had all my wording down and I knew what I was going to say. He looked at me and smiled that award-winning smile that melted my heart every time. It was then, right then in the exact place where we met, I wanted to tell him. I needed to tell him. It wasn't the way I planned it, but I knew it was right.

I stood, and he looked at me. I straddled the low cement wall we were sitting on and faced him. He mimicked my move. I placed both of his hands in mine. I looked deep into those big brown eyes of his. My heart soared with all the joy and excitement of a Christmas morning.

"Peter, it only seems fitting to tell you here, at the very spot where we met. I don't just love you for who you are, but I am in love with you. I cannot even begin to tell you how grateful I am to you for showing me again that love is possible and how beautiful it can be. I know I am and will forever be in love with you," I said, my voice full of heartfelt emotion.

"Jeffrey, my dear sweet Jeffrey," he responded, his voice breaking a little. "I didn't think it was possible to find someone like you. I am in love with you, and have been for some time now. I was just a bit afraid to tell you."

It was just that simple and sweet. Nothing as I planned—it wasn't necessary to follow that script. It was better the way it happened. It matched the tempo of our relationship—simple and sweet. We enjoyed the way things were going between us. It was a natural progression—nothing forced no pressure.

"The moment to tell you was right, right then," I said.

He smiled, touched the side of my face, and said, "I can't believe you. You went through all this. The dinner, all the planning. You are incredible,"

"Well, the night is full of surprises. We were on time, the dinner was set up, me just blurting out the 'I love you' thing, which I do. So far, everything is going well. I hope you are enjoying it. I hope you won't be embarrassed," I said.

"Why would I be embarrassed?" he asked.

"Us, you and I, dinner for two, with a private waiter, here in a lakeside park with people passing by," I replied, unsure of how he would react to everything I planned.

"That doesn't concern me," he assured me. "Don't let it concern you."

"Good! Now I can relax," I sighed heavily.

"Yeah, we both can. I have to say, I didn't know what to expect. I have wanted to tell you that I love you for a week or two now. I was getting a bit stressed. Then the other morning, Gabby walked in on our brunch. I was a little on edge, with everything that has been going on," he explained.

"I could tell. I was actually going to tell you then. I am kind of glad I didn't. I like this setting better," I said with a smile.

"Me, too. The place we met and dinner at the lake. Brilliant, just brilliant," he responded.

Greg approached with the champagne. He filled our glasses and let us know the progress of the meal. He told us that the steak was just about done and we should probably think about heading over to the table.

"Nice friend you have there, to do all this for you," Peter commented.

"He is. I love him to death. He is getting well-compensated for his time," I said.

"OH?" Peter raised an eyebrow questioningly and totally in jest.

"Don't be silly. Nothing would ever happen between Greg and me. He actually insisted on doing all of this for nothing. I wouldn't hear of it. So I am giving him two tickets to fly his boyfriend and him on vacation," I said.

"Sweet!" Peter said.

"Yeah, so is he," I added.

We had dinner. Greg did everything up right. He thought of everything. He was amazing. I pitched the idea to him and just asked for suggestions and he took the ball and ran with it. He elaborated on the idea and added some special touches. His attention to detail was exquisite—nothing was left to chance.

At the end of dinner, we offered to help clean things up and pack things away. Greg declined our offer and told us that he was going to surprise his boyfriend and he was on the way. He had planned a little evening of romance for himself. We waited for Marc to arrive, which was only twenty minutes after Peter and I finished. I thanked Greg for everything, as did Peter, and we left the two of them alone.

We were basking in the romantic glow of the evening. The evening was going nicely. I was very pleased with everything. There was one other surprise. It was as much for me as it was for him. My anticipation for what was about to happen mounted with each step I took. We walked the path home shoulder to shoulder, smiling.

I was feeling the electricity and excitement build in me. I was about to jump out of my skin. Every nerve ending was on high alert. My anticipation was mounting at high velocity. I kept looking at him; I felt he knew the evening wasn't over yet. If he knew what was ahead, he didn't lead on to knowing. It was probably me, knowing what was planned and what I had in mind.

When we were in the condo, he settled onto the couch and made himself at home. I liked that about him. Ever since I first met him, he had been secure in himself and with us. He was just himself, no facades. He made being with him easy. I watched him from the kitchen, as I readied phase two of the evening.

"Hey!" he called out. "What are you doing in there? Come in and join me on the couch."

"Can't, Peter. I am kinda busy right now. I'll only be a second or two longer. Stay where you are—the night isn't over yet," I explained.

"Really?!" he asked excitedly.

"Really," I answered, finishing up my preparations.

I rushed about, getting the silver serving tray, champagne glasses, and bowl of strawberries out of the refrigerator. I had set the small crock-pot on low to melt the chocolate. It was melted creamy smooth and warm.

I needed to distract him while I finished in the other two rooms. It wasn't going to be easy.

I walked into the living room and headed directly towards him. He looked up at me and smiled. I stopped dead in my tracks. That gaze and smile of his was polarizing. My heart went into some rapid arrhythmia. I felt my eyes begin to tear up. This man affected me as no other had in the past. I was still astounded that he was in love with me. How did I get so lucky?

I stood there looking down at him. I didn't move a muscle. I couldn't. I was transfixed on the gorgeous man who was sitting on my couch. None of the crap about the Austin deal mattered right now. The only thing important was that I loved him deeply—so deeply that it almost hurt. It was a good hurt.

"What is it, Jeff?" His voiced pierced the silence, as he began to stand.

"NO! Don't get up. It's nothing. I got caught up on a thought and I'm just extremely happy," I said as I moved towards him. I leaned down and kissed him lightly on the forehead. "Now you have to do me a favor."

"Alright, sure. What?" he asked.

"I am not quite finished with something yet. Here, let me remove your shoes and I want you to lie back and keep your eyes closed. Don't cheat and peek! I will only be a couple of minutes more, I promise. Trust me on this," I said.

I removed his shoes and swung his legs up on the couch. He closed his eyes and lay prone with his arms crossed over his chest. He was so damn handsome. I could have just stood and looked at him the entire evening. I couldn't, though. I tore myself away to complete my mission.

I scurried between the kitchen and bedroom a couple of times. I had an assortment of candles and incense (a bit retro sixties, but it worked) arranged on the heat register, dresser, chairs, and the tables in the room. The lights were completely off, with the exception of one can light behind a floor plant.

I arranged the silver tray on the bed, with two champagne glasses, the bowl of strawberries on ice, and the melted chocolate in the warmer. I stripped all the bedding away, with the exception of the satin bottom sheet and pillows. Numerous fragrances began to saturate the room. The bedroom was set—next was the bath.

I had installed a large Jacuzzi tub when I remodeled the bathroom. After lighting the candles that were arranged around the edge of the tub and room, I made a quick inspection of the setting I was trying to create. Hanging from a couple of hooks on the wall were two short silk robes and boxers for afterwards. I began to fill the tub and started the jets. I returned to the bedroom to get the glasses off the tray and shut the door. Everything was set.

Taking a deep, relaxing inhale, I wandered back into the living room. I extracted an envelope from my computer desk. There were no markings on it, nothing to designate who the recipient was. There was only one recipient, and he remained on the couch as instructed. I was getting more anxious by the second.

I came up alongside the couch arm and knelt. I laid the envelope on the couch table, in place until the right delivery time. Grabbing the stereo remote, I started the music. I was setting my plan in motion.

"AHHH! You are back. I was getting lonely," he said quietly.

"Yeah, I am here. It is just you and me, mister," I spoke softly.

"What have you been doing?" he playfully inquired.

"Stuff," I said, starting to massage his temples.

"Hmmm," was all he murmured. His eyes were still closed.

"I have something for you. You can open your eyes now," I said, laying the envelope in his hands.

I stood as he took the envelope and inspected it. I walked down the hall to the bath. I heard the envelope flap being released as I shut the door. The note I wrote was now open. I stripped and submerged myself into the tub. The note was pretty simple. It was an expression of my feelings and my growing love for him. It also gave him a clue as to what was awaiting him.

Peter,

Since the day I first met you, my days are brighter, my life is fuller. I didn't think it was possible to feel the things that I feel again. I see things in a different light, your light. You have touched my soul and heart. I love you.

Jeffrey

P.S. 6N2 = tonight. I will be waiting in the Jacuzzi.

The only light was that of the glowing candles, warm and soothing. I held his glass of champagne and waited. I set mine on the edge of the tub. I was propped up against the wall of the tub, listening carefully. I didn't hear him moving in the hall, but I knew he was there. I watched the door, my heart beating so fast and hard that I thought it was going to pound out of my chest.

I saw the doorknob turn and the door swing in. I looked up at him, and he was smiling. I raised his glass and winked at him. He didn't say a word; he just fixed his deliberate gaze on me and began to unbutton his shirt.

I sat in the tub and sipped my champagne, still holding his glass. He slowly and seductively removed his clothing, allowing it to lie where it dropped. He turned his back to me and slowly lowered the waistband of his briefs, sliding them over his bum and down his thighs. Stepping out of them, he turned and walked to the tub. Grabbing his glass from me, he lowered himself into the water.

He situated himself between my legs and leaned back against me. I encircled his chest and waist. He relaxed his head back and laid it beside mine, on my shoulder. We lay there with our eyes closed. I caressed his chest and abdomen, while he caressed my outer thighs and legs. We lay entwined for a while and let the jets massage our bodies. Little was said, though we communicated volumes with our touches and embraces.

I turned my head slightly. "I am so in love with you. You are an incredible man. Thanks for being you and thanks for letting me love you," I said, expressing my sincere feelings.

"You make that easy to do. My live is enriched because of you, Jeffrey," he replied.

We lingered in the tub for a while longer. The sensation of his fingertips moving against my skin sent bolts of excitement throughout my entire body. I held him tightly and massaged his torso periodically. I allowed my hands to roam down his stomach and between his legs to his inner thighs and up again.

The water was beginning to cool down, and we needed to leave the soothing aquatic oasis. Everything was set up in the next room. I wanted him there. I wanted the evening to progress. He didn't appear to be anxious or even to have the slightest urgency. He knew what was eventually going to transpire and he was as laid-back as he always is. His calm balanced my anxiousness.

Nestling my face in the curve of his neck, I kissed him lightly. He responded by gripping my outer thigh and squeezing tenderly. My lips roamed up to his ear. I suggested that we get up and dry off. He leaned forward and gave me room to stand. I took the glass from his hand and set it on the side of the tub. He stood and faced me. Our eyes locked, fixed. Our stare was a prelude to an embrace filled with passion.

Breaking our embrace, I started the shower, and we rinsed off quickly. Turning off the shower, I reached for a towel and began to glide it over his skin. We stepped out of the tub and I completed drying him off. I handed him the silk boxers and robe. I finished drying off as he combed his damp hair and dressed. I followed suit, then took his hand and led him towards the bedroom.

We reached the bedroom door, where he paused a moment and looked at me. It was as if he was making sure this was the right thing to do and the right time. His look was filled with reassurance, tenderness, and affection. His facial expression conveyed that it was the right moment to share ourselves completely and physically express our love and desire.

I opened the door. The room was aglow with soft flickers of candlelight. The incense fragrance filled the room. The champagne bucket with a chilled bottle, strawberries, and chocolate was centered on the bed, the tray shimmering in the candlelight. He looked around the room while he held my hand. We walked to the window, vertical blinds open and the view rich in moonlight.

I went back into the bathroom and retrieved the glasses from the tub. Filling both of them, I handed him one as I approached the window to be by his side.

"It's been a wonderful evening, thanks. You have made me feel so special," Peter softly said.

"It has been nice, and you are very special to me," I agreed.

With that short exchange, he drew me near. Our bodies pressed tightly and firmly together. There was a passion in his embrace and kiss that I had not experienced that was a bit different from the others we had shared. I loved him and he loved me. We were going to share the physical love, and the passion was mounting as we embraced.

He stepped back. We stood in front of the window. It was dark both inside and out. The candles gave off a low glow, just enough light to see each other, but not enough to let others see inside. He reached for the tie of my robe and pulled it loose. My robe fell open, and his hands glided along my waist and onto my chest, then up to my shoulders and under the fabric of the robe. He pushed the robe off my shoulders, and it slid down my arms and fell to the floor. I followed his lead, and he was soon standing in only the silk boxers.

We stood there kissing and caressing. I guided him to the bed. He stepped backwards to the edge and sat down. As I leaned forward and kissed him passionately, he began to lie back. His arms enveloped me as we lowered ourselves flat, and I lay on top of him. His hands explored every inch of me that was within his reach. We grinded our groins together, separated only by the thin silk fabric.

Raising up and peering into his eyes, I felt overtaken with love, desire, and lust. I lowered again, and our lips met. I was receptive to his oral advance. I shivered with exhilaration, as his tongue trailed along the backside of my teeth and then outlined my lips. He then trailed along my jaw, nibbled on my earlobe, and darted his tongue in and around my inner ear. Working his way towards my forehead, with soft and gentle kisses, he paused just long enough to gently kiss my eyelids, and the bridge of my nose. He then returned to his starting point and continued to passionately explore my mouth. Our kiss was sending me into a frenzy of excitement.

His strong hands slid under the elastic waistband of my boxers, stroking and taunting my flesh. I started my own assault, sucking and licking my way to his ear and then down his neck to his chest. My tongue never lost contact with his skin, as I worked over each of his nipples. He arched his back in pleasure and moaned softly, as he fell victim to my deliberate advances. I wanted his whole body. I wanted him to experience a level of ecstasy he had never felt before. I would work at sending him there. His pleasure was my mission.

Moving down to his pelvic area, I ran my hands inside the legs of the boxers and up to the waistband. From the inside, I secured the band in my hands and slowly pulled it down, over his hips. He lifted his hips slightly to allow the garment easy movement. As the silk boxers slid across his pelvis and down his thighs, he raised his legs to allow their removal. Once he was naked and lying there full exposed, I stood and slowly stripped mine off. He was noticeably aroused and excited.

I returned to the bed, and he remained on his back. I lay down on my side next to him and started to run my fingertips over his warm and moist flesh. I reached over him, dipped a strawberry into the chocolate, and fed it to him. As he chewed the sweet fruit, I submerged another into the chocolate and allowed the creamy brown liquid to drizzle on his chest, especially his nipple. I bent over and licked the concoction up, sucking lightly on his erect nipple. He shuddered slightly and exhaled deeply.

I reached to the bottom of the bowl and secured a chilled berry. I bit into it so that half remained. I took the sweet fruit and traced his erection with it. I then dipped my fingers into the chocolate and smeared it over his penis head. Holding him at the base, I started to lick him clean. His moans were audible and his pleasure was visible. He gyrated his hips as I lovingly engulfed him.

He reached down and ran his hands through my hair. I took a minute or two to give him a little more delight before I returned to his side. We then became entwined in each other's arms and legs again. I started to lean back and was reminded that the tray was still in the middle of the bed. I broke away for a moment, not only to move the tray, but also to slow down a bit and make the moment last.

"Don't take those too far away," he panted.

"Only to the nightstand—they are within your reach. Sooooo, the sweets are more appealing?" I quipped.

"You are so extremely handsome and desirable, that bowl of fruit is NOT what I want. I just may want to have a little fun with that chocolate," he said with a smile.

With the tray settled on the nightstand, he reached for my hand, and I extended it to him. He tugged me back to the bed, and we picked up where we left off. We now had the full expanse of the bed and were unlimited in our movements.

Peter molded me into a position that allowed us to share in mutual gratification. He expertly sent me into spasms of enjoyment, masterfully fondling and orally satisfying my senses. He took me to a point of orgasm and then suspended his assault. There was no doubt in my mind that we would be repeating our activities again this evening, but we wanted to enjoy the first full-scale encounter to the fullest.

I wanted him, all of him. I wanted to feel, smell, and taste every inch of the man I felt such deep love and respect for. Passion mounted as we explored each other's flesh. He grabbed my wrists and held my hands over my head as he lowered his body to mine. I spread my legs to allow his pelvis to grind against mine. He centered himself on top of me, the full weight of his body against mine. He again started nibbling on my earlobe and darted his tongue in and out of my inner ear. I was going insane. He found one of my most sensitive and stimulating spots and was taking me to a pitch of ecstasy and excitement that I had never experienced. I clung on to the sheets and my body went rigid, as he worked his magic on me, and guided us through that magical carpet ride of pleasure.

I raised my legs and wrapped them around his buttocks and thighs. I locked my ankles together and squeezed him tightly. I wanted him close, as close as I could physically get him. He looked deep into my eyes and released my wrists. His hands roamed along my side and up along the backside of my thighs. He then held my face in his hands and kissed me softly, yet firmly. He knelt back on his knees, while his hands wandered over my chest and down my abdomen.

He slowly stroked my erection and cupped my testicles as he stared at me. I was lost in his touch and the enjoyment he was delivering. I reached for him, and he responded by laying back down on top of me. We submerged again into the throes of passion, and my urgency to have him inside of me took over. I wanted all of him, in every way I could have him.

"Peter, I need and want you to make love to me," I insisted.

He said nothing, just smiled and raised up on his elbows, responding with a touch and kiss. He then reached between my legs and ran a finger between my scrotum and anus—my most favorite and sensitive G-spot. He again knelt between my legs as he rotated his finger in a circular motion. I raised my legs up and rested my heels on his shoulders. I lay there, surrendering myself to him and his touch. I applied some lube to his erection and slowly stroked it. He added it to his fingers and continued to fondle me. He inserted a finger, adding to the pleasure that he was already giving me.

It had been a long time since I had engaged in this act. I would need to be properly prepared and relaxed. He must have sensed this, as he was taking his time to do just that, adequately getting me ready for what was to come. I wanted him as much as he wanted me.

The foreplay was fantastic. He sent me into realms of ecstasy with just his touch. I had not felt this type of mounting pleasure in years. He expertly manipulated my body with his hands and mouth. I was doing my best to reciprocate.

The time came, and I was ready. He leaned back, rolled a condom on, and applied more lube. I reached between us and rolled his testicles in my fingers as he completed his final preparations. I felt him position his erection and slowly insert himself into me. He slowly penetrated me. I was fully aware of his length and girth as he managed to submerge himself fully. He was tender and caring as he entered me.

I inhaled deeply, and he stopped. I assured him it was pleasure and not pain that caused my reaction. I brought him down close to me and kissed him. He responded with a slow and methodical rocking. He adjusted my legs on his shoulders and continued to slide himself deep inside of me. He would slowly withdraw and then penetrate me deeply again. He repeated this motion as I continued to meet his thrusts with raising my hips in the same rhythm.

He took his time to make sure that our first interlude of lovemaking lasted a long time. His pleasure was obvious, as was mine. His rhythm became more urgent, and his breath was getting harder and shorter. I was sure he was on the edge of orgasm. I was close as well.

He completely withdrew and rolled the condom off. He began to masturbate along with me, and we were going to ejaculate together. He began to get a contorted look on his face, and I began to convulse as my orgasm rocketed into the air. His hot, streaming jets flew across my stomach and chest. We were gasping for air as our eruptions continued. Our eyes were fixed on each other, as we became fully spent. Slowly, he lay down on top of me as our hot, creamy fluid gelled together and slowly drizzled down the side of my waist.

Still panting heavily, all I could say was, "Holy fuck, that was great!"

"Yeah! Holy fuck is right. WOW!" he returned.

"You were absolutely incredible," I said breathlessly.

"I didn't enjoy it at all," he humorously teased.

"Come to think of it, I didn't much care for it, either. Maybe we are doing it wrong," I joked back.

"Well, if that was wrong, I can't wait to see what happens when we get it right!" he panted.

We lay spent for a few minutes, neither of us making a move. We were absorbing the full sensation of the lovemaking we had just completed. We shared some tender afterplay, once we regained our breath, and then we showered. The shower jets tingled our skin, which was hypersensitive from the heightened sensitivity of lovemaking.

Once out of the shower, we returned to the bed and into each other's arms. We spoke softly and melted together in our embrace. We exchanged expressions of love and spoke of how blissfully happy we were. I rolled gently onto my side and faced him. He looked over at me and smiled. I could never get enough of that.

He was so handsome and sweet. SWEET—that was what our relationship was. I was beginning to become overwhelmed with emotion again. He truly fulfilled me. I couldn't find the words right then to express what I was feeling to him. I just hugged him and held him tight.

In my private time, when I sat alone thinking, I often thought about how intense my feelings for this man had become. On one hand, it scared me and I questioned whether it was actually possible to be in love so quickly. On the other, I knew that he filled the void of emotional emptiness that ached inside of me. I know I was being a hopeless romantic where he was concerned, but was I actually looking at what was happening with open eyes and feet firmly planted on the ground?

I knew I had deep-seated feelings for him. I had to trust my instincts and allow my heart to lead me in right direction, where he and the relationship that developed between us were concerned. I couldn't deny that we shared an indisputable bond. I was overanalyzing, and I needed to relax and enjoy what was happening. When I allowed myself the luxury of total openness to him and what I was feeling, I was completely comfortable with the place to which we had evolved so far. I wondered, at times, if he struggled with any of the same thoughts.

I wasn't having any of those conflicting thoughts as I lay next to him. I was in a realm of total bliss. I was feeling emotionally satisfied and physically stimulated. The intensity of our lovemaking renewed and awakened all my senses. I felt so alive and euphoric.

"It seems that you are ready to go again, mister," he said, as he felt my arousal pressing against his hip.

"You have that effect on me. You have since we met. So, it is all your fault," I explained.

"I accept full responsibility. What will my penance be?" he asked playfully.

"A repeat performance," I said with a smile.

"If I must," he said, giving me an exasperated sigh.

He rolled against me, and we began to celebrate our newly verbalized love again. The second round was even better than the first. We explored different aspects of our lovemaking and found different levels of ecstasy we hadn't experienced the first time. We took our time and shared in the delivery of pleasure. These intensely sustained actions lasted into the early hours of the morning. When we were totally spent, we fell asleep completely satisfied.

I woke up to the phone ringing. I ignored it and let the voice mail pick it up. I did get up to start the coffee and shower. Peter stirred a bit, but remained in bed. I was in the kitchen when I heard the shower and knew that he was up and moving. He finished his shower and joined me in the living room, carrying the coffee I left on the vanity for him.

I felt his nakedness press against me as we stood looking out the window at the lake. We stood there molded together, his right arm around my waist. I rested my head against his shoulder. Our silent communication of physical closeness was all that was needed.

It was a lazy morning, and we repeated the activities of the prior evening. There was no urgency to end our time together. We had a couple of social commitments that day—lunch with a couple of my friends and dinner at his parents'. I could have spent the whole day locked up inside with him. He said so as well, and we contemplated canceling our plans, but decided against that. We had a great day together, which only complemented the evening the night before.

CHAPTER 8

Fall

It was no surprise to me when Peter showed up at my door. I had grown accustomed to him being there or me being up north at his house. In the days and weeks after we consummated our relationship, we enjoyed a series of rendezvous and stolen moments. The deal in Austin was heating up. Work for me was getting busy as well. We took our time together seriously, concentrating on quality of time and not the limited quantity of it.

On one particular evening that was not spent in loving, tender embraces, we had to have an emotionally raw and explicit conversation about Austin. We had to revisit the possibility of him accepting the offer, his moving, my involvement, and the reality of us not being as we had become.

It was an intense conversation. Emotions, especially frustration, were running at high pitch. We didn't argue and it wasn't a fight, but it was a highly charged emotional debate. We were looking at the situation from two different viewpoints. Our feelings for each other were a liability and not an asset.

Peter's viewpoint was a simple one. We loved each other, we wanted to be together, and we should be. He would be making enough money on the deal to support us both. I could quit my job and move, find another, or I could step down from my management position and return to flying. I could commute from Austin and retain my employment with a company I had many years of service with. I listened intently to his plans. He had a total of four scenarios. He had obviously put some thought into the solutions he was confident would work.

I agreed that his plans were workable, but there were a few things from my point of view that needed to be considered. I laid them out for him. It wasn't easy to discuss. I was concerned that it was all so new for us, and our relationship had been short. My family would be closer if I remained in Chicago. My mother was alone and since my father died, I needed to be close—at least closer than Austin.

There was also the matter of my seniority. If I were to move, I would have to return to flying, and that would be out of a base that meant working weekends. My seniority was better in Chicago, and that meant I would be commuting, which added to my time away from him.

I was mainly concerned with the length of time of our relationship. That was the big concern for me. I was probably being a bit overly cautious, but it was a factor. I tried to express this to him without hurting him. I told him that if we had been together for a year or more, this conversation wouldn't be taking place. I would have already been packed.

Something inside of me was hesitating. I couldn't place a finger on what it was. That inner voice kept telling me not to do it right now. Wait—if it is meant to be, it will evolve that way. I couldn't explain it to anyone. I barely understood it myself. I tried to tell the girls at work, my mother, and my best friend Michael, and couldn't put it into words that made any sense. I got mixed reviews from them all. I only knew that it was this enormous feeling inside of me, one I couldn't shake, as much as I tried. It was pulling me away from being impulsive and going with my heart. It wasn't easy to talk about. I am sure it wasn't easy for him to hear.

That evening, we discussed everything related to us and tried to reach a compromise. We agreed to see each other as much as possible, but agreed it would not be a commuting relationship. This is where I had to laugh. *"It isn't going to be a commuting relationship?"* I wondered to myself. It would be a relationship that used planes instead of cars, included two different cities and approximately fifteen hundred miles of travel, but we aren't going to call it a long-distance or commuting relationship. Now, it smelled like, felt like, and had all the indications of a commuting, long-distance relationship. But I wasn't willing to give up on us. I was willing to try anything, except moving to Austin. I was not completely sure why, but something inside was telling me now was not the time to move. It was all so confusing and such a conflict for me.

We agreed on no time limits or expectations—we would allow it to form and evolve as it would. I would travel when I could, and he would as he could. I understood his frustration and his desire to have some sort of solid foundation for us. I wanted that as well, but there just wasn't a way to achieve that, with all the variables in play.

We went to bed that night emotionally and mentally spent. He laid his head on my shoulder and his arm across my chest. I cradled him in close. We were silent, other than the "I love you" we exchanged before drifting off.

That night was difficult for us, but nothing like the night when I answered the door and instantly knew something was wrong. The look in his eyes told the whole story. He had just returned from a short two-day trip to Austin. He came directly from the airport to me.

"Hey, mister. How was the trip?" I asked. "You look…well, I am not sure how you look. Handsome as ever, but something is up."

"Sorry for not calling last night. We ran late and then there were dinner reservations. Bill and I were obligated to attend. It was a bit overwhelming. I thought of you the whole time I was there and wished that you were there with me," he said soberly.

"You look conflicted. Need a shower and a drink or a couch and a shrink?" I quipped, trying to remain lighthearted.

"All of the above," he answered flatly.

"Well, you know where the shower is. I will get you something to change into, unless you have clothes with you. What's your poison?" I asked.

"I will decide in the shower, but I will need something comfortable to change into," he said.

I followed him into the bathroom. I took his suit as he stripped out of it and stepped into the shower. I hung his clothes up and got him something to put on. I quickly went through the house, lowered the lights, and lit candles. I put some soft and smooth jazz on the stereo. I was trying to create a calming atmosphere. I sensed and felt that it was a must.

When he entered the living room, he looked revitalized—physically, anyway. His eyes told a different story. I took the liberty to pour a glass of wine for him, and he grabbed it off the coffee table as he walked up to me and just hugged me tightly.

"Let's sit," I suggested.

"No, let's go lie down and be close," he countered.

"Ok, mister," I complied. "I am right behind you."

"I want to know that I made the right decision, that I didn't fuck up," he said.

With that, he held my hand and led us into the bedroom. I wasn't sure what that last comment meant. It concerned me. Was it about the deal or getting involved with me?

I didn't say a word as I followed him into the bedroom. We propped ourselves up on pillows and got comfortable. He was so close to me, you couldn't slide a credit card between us. I could feel his pulse with every beat of his heart. I remained silent. He would talk when he was ready.

He softly spoke. "I signed the papers. I sold my business. Bill and I agreed that the offer was too good to turn down."

"Shouldn't we be celebrating? I am so happy for you. This is what you wanted and you have worked for. I'm excited. Why the funk? What has you so bothered and pensive?" I asked.

"Yes, the deal is what I wanted," he began. "It is a good deal—a great one, actually. Bill did a good job on my behalf. I was all hyped about it yesterday in final negotiations and this morning when I actually signed the papers. The plane ride home was when I started thinking about the personal side of it all and the impact it will have on my mom, dad, my sisters, and especially you—what this will do to us. I like us and what we have become. I am afraid it will all be lost now. Did I just sell my relationship with you away, too? There will be little time for us here. I want you there with me. I don't want to lose you or leave you behind." He stopped his thoughts abruptly.

"Peter, my sweet, adorable Peter. We have been through all of this already. I promised I would be in Austin and we would make things work somehow for now. I'm not going to allow you to discard me like yesterday's newspaper. You know my position and we talked it all out. I am not going away," I said.

"That was before it was reality. Now that it is, are you sure you feel the same way?" he asked.

"Ten thousand percent. I won't allow you to bike into my life and abruptly leave. It would be unfair to both of us. I don't have the answers to how this whole thing is going to affect us. The distance thing is only a speed bump in the road for us. Everything will fall into place as it is meant to," I reassured him.

"Nice to hear. Thanks," he said.

"Have you told the family yet? Or just told Gabby and let her run with it, like the newswire?" I joked, trying to interject a little humor.

"Yeah, they know. I am—or should I say, we are—having breakfast with my parents in the morning. Bill will be there, too," he explained.

"Me?" I asked.

"Yeah, we are all involved in this somehow, and it was my decision that I wanted you all as informed as Bill and me. Bill will run through everything," he confirmed.

There was no reason to dispute the decision. It was arranged, and I knew that I couldn't change his mind. I needed to be there to show my support and to fortify my conviction of keeping us together.

Breakfast was interesting, to say the least. Bill and Peter did the majority of the talking, and his parents asked all the questions. They were exchanging thoughts and ideas. His parents were more interested in his welfare and making sure that there was no way he could be taken advantage of. SCREWED, as his father put it.

The four of them were very business savvy. I sat quietly, just taking it all in and listening. His mother would pat my leg from time to time. She would then shoot me a warm, comforting smile. His family and I had a mutual affection for one another, which had been cultivated in the short time Peter and I had been involved.

His parents asked some tough questions. They had his best interests at heart and wanted to be sure it was a good business deal. I was lost in my thoughts, trying to absorb all the details. It sounded very good. I could see why Peter was so excited about the deal.

I also understood why Peter was so concerned and conflicted. He built his life in the city he grew up in and had never lived this far from home before. His opportunities were always within the city limits, so he didn't need to move away. His family was extremely important to him and he would be leaving, for the first time, the comfort zone and security he had built for himself. It was a big step and move for him.

I understood his parent's apprehension. His parents were not making the decision for him—they would never do that. They were playing devil's advocate and trying to look at all aspects of the proposal. It was important to Peter that they were comfortable with his decision.

"Jeff? Hey, Jeffrey," Peter said, staring at me.

"What? Sorry, was a little lost there in thought. I was trying to absorb all this," I replied.

"What do you think? What are your thoughts? Any questions?" Bill asked.

"Well, it all sounds great and pretty solid to me. I'm excited for him. No questions, really. Most of them have been answered already. Well, I guess I do have one," I said.

"Let's have it, mister," Peter said, looking a bit concerned.

"When does all this take place?" I asked.

I felt a bit selfish, asking that question. I just wanted to know how much time I had left before he was gone. I knew the deal was good or they wouldn't have considered it and signed the agreement. There was a "termination of deal" clause built into the contract. I just wanted to know when it was actually going to be finalized.

Bill and Peter tag teamed the answer. They both explained how the time frame worked. As it stood now, possession would be in January. That is when the deal would be final and there would be no backing out. Things could change prior to that.

With breakfast finished, we all went our separate ways. Peter and I arrived at his office. It was open, and everyone looked busy. I told Peter I would wait upstairs so he could have the time with his employees, who were also his friends. I actually wanted him to drop me off at the train, but he insisted that I stay.

I was on the deck reflecting on the morning's conversation. I didn't hear him enter through the bedroom French doors. I was completely lost in thought, and he startled me.

"How did that go?" I asked.

"Well, they are a great group. I have kept them informed, and nothing was a surprise. I told them their jobs were protected and they would be offered a severance package, if they didn't want to work for the new bosses. I had to tell them that I wouldn't be involved with the department they would be working in when the deal was final. That was tough. They had a lot of questions. We decided that we would have dinner this evening and talk everything out," he explained.

"I think that is a great idea. You need that time with them. Will I see you tomorrow, then?" I asked.

"Tomorrow? You are going tonight. They want you to come along," he said.

"You need your private time with them. I am not going this evening, and please, no arguments or discussion. It is important that they, as well as you, have face-to-face time. This will be difficult for all of you. You love and care about them. It wouldn't be right to have me there. I appreciate that you all want me there, but it should be only the four of you," I said.

"All right, I understand your position on this. I agree with your logic and thoughtfulness. I think they will appreciate the time alone with me. I will see you afterwards. I will come down and spend the night. Give me a second—I want to check on something. I'll be right back," he said.

"OK. Hurry back," I replied.

Peter returned in about fifteen minutes. I looked up to see him standing in the threshold of the doorway. He was giving me a devilish smile and gestured with his finger for me to come and join him inside.

"We didn't get the opportunity to get reacquainted last night," he said, as he started to unbutton my shirt. "I need to make that up to you."

"The boss is playing hooky. What will the employees think?" I joked.

"I gave them the day off and sent them home. They deserve the time off," he said.

Peter and I made love for an hour or two, and then he dropped me off at the train station. He needed to get ready for their early dinner, and I wanted to get prepared for an evening alone with him. I was getting used to having him around. Any questions or doubts I was having about being in love with him so quickly were fading. I just wished I could shake the unsettling feeling I had about moving to Austin and pack up and move with him. But I just couldn't. I remained guarded about it.

The next couple of weeks flew by. The deal in Austin was finalized, and only one thing changed—they wanted possession on November first. I didn't understand why, but I am not business savvy and was sure that it made some sense somehow. Peter would have to be there on November first as well. I hated that. I had just lost two months. He was upset about that, too.

I was extremely upset about it, the more I thought about it. There wasn't any time to get used to the idea of him being gone. One might argue that it was better that way, without a long, drawn-out good-bye. I was unsettled about not having any time left. Time would be at a premium and a priority.

Peter had told me about the company in Austin and told me they were a parent company of many of the brands and products that I used everyday. I started my own personal boycott of them and their products. It was my own personal campaign to stick it to them, as I put it. Peter just laughed at me when I told him. He tried to reason with me about my boycott, saying that it would probably have little effect on their bottom line. I didn't care—it was the principle that mattered.

I agreed to back away from one part of my boycotting campaign, during one of my rants to him about the possession date. I agreed that a letter campaign would not be in his best interest and that I wouldn't send any letters to the CEO of the parent company. I think he was relieved and grateful.

Bill tried to get the date changed back to January. From what I was told, it seemed to be a heated debate between them and Austin. It was almost a deal-breaker. Selfishly, I was hoping that it was. I felt awful about how I was thinking, but it was caused by the way I felt. Bill and Peter decided that the deal was so good that they conceded to the date change.

Time being the precious commodity that it was, I changed some vacation time around and spent his last week in town with him. That week was rough for the two of us. Our emotions were running in high gear. There were farewell parties to attend, time dedicated to his family, and the dreaded packing of the personal items.

The movers would pack everything up and do all the moving. He wanted to pack up some of the more sentimental items himself. We had to sit down and figure out a day or night when he could dedicate time for just that. That night was particularly difficult.

I was the go-get-this and will-you-get-me-that guy that evening. We dedicated an entire evening just to packing some of his personal belongings. I actually didn't do any of the packing—that was all his to do. I was there for a specific purpose: moral support. I had my duties, limited as they were, but I took them seriously. I sat there watching as he collected memorabilia from shelves and cabinets, arranging it on the living room floor.

He would stop and look at each piece and remember the memory attached. It was like watching him relive parts of his life. He shared a story about something once in a while, but for the most part he was silent.

He had filled a box and started to tape it shut. He set the tape gun down and stood with his arms folded in front of him, his back to me. He just gazed down at the full box, and I could feel the pain he was experiencing at the moment. I got up from my chair and walked up behind him. I wrapped my arms around his folded arms and just held him. He was quiet, and then his upper torso started to shake slightly. I realized that he was gently weeping.

"Have I made a mistake, mister?" he quietly spoke. "I'm feeling pretty awful right now and thinking I have."

"Seller's remorse? Remorse over leaving your family and friends? It is only natural for you to feel those things. They are part of your life and who you are. This is a new adventure, a new chapter in your life. I am sure you are going to have some apprehension, some mixed feelings," I said.

"I am missing this already," he said, as he tightened his grip on my arm, referring to him and me.

"I'm not going anywhere. I'm just exchanging my mode of travel. Instead of a train, it will be a plane. We will have this. Not much is changing. I promise," I said. It was a promise to him and me.

We stood there in silence and remained in the embrace. I memorized the feeling of his body against mine. I cataloged every inch of it in my memory. I stood there with the side of my face flat against his back; arms wrapped around him, and took in his every essence. When I moved my face up and around to the back of his neck, his aroma assaulted my sense of smell. It was his scent, that unique fragrance we all possess. It stopped my movement immediately. I inhaled deeply. It was a beautiful cocktail of his freshly washed hair, his skin, and his favorite cologne. My olfactory senses were diligently storing the potpourri of scents. They were all his and I wanted to commit them to memory.

Sensing that he needed some sort of distraction and diversion from the packing, I suggested a union break. He agreed and said that he would go make some coffee and return shortly. I was sure that he was a bundle of nerves and his emotions were running wild.

He was thinking about all he was leaving behind and would miss. I was sure that he had some anxiety over what to expect and what would be expected of him in Austin. His eyes were telling the whole story. They darted around and would not remain fixed on anything for long. You could tell his mind was on overdrive.

When he returned from the kitchen, two steaming cups of coffee in hand, he looked around at all the stuff remaining on the floor. Almost immediately, you could see the tenseness well up in him. I suggested that he join me for a minute on the couch. He did and settled in right next to me.

"Hear me out. Indulge me for a minute," I stated, just to get his attention. "I know you are feeling overwhelmed. So much is changing in your world and you have had little or no time to prepare. There are people and things and a comfort zone you are leaving behind. You are amped out. There are also new beginnings and adventures ahead for you. This is a goal you have set for yourself and have achieved. That is something to celebrate and to be proud of. The people and things left behind will be there. Your family, friends, and all those you love and who love you are behind you and support you in this endeavor. Change is not always easy, but we are constantly changing, every day and every minute. You are walking a path that was written for you, that you helped write and you elected to walk. You know this is the right thing. It was the right choice to make," I said.

"You simply amaze me," he said with a smile. "I have been struggling with all that, especially tonight, probably because of the packing. Thanks for understanding and being here."

"Peter, do you know how proud everyone is of you? You have such a great support system—your parents, your sisters, and all the others. You are truly blessed to have the people around you that you do. I completely understand why you are feeling the way you do. But isn't it absolutely wonderful knowing that they all are in your corner?" I asked.

He was serious as he looked at me and said, "What about you? It is all of this and how it pertains to and plays out for you that really concerns me."

"I know that you have been concerned with how this is going to affect us," I said. "I am not going anywhere. I made a promise to you. We have discussed it all and I will not be detoured from it. I am committed to our plan and to you. Please let that be the least of your concerns. I will be in charge of us and you take care of the rest. Deal?"

"Deal. I find myself more enamored with you every day. You make all of this easier and yet so difficult. It scares me—thinking of leaving you behind simply scares me. I am afraid that we will never have the opportunity to see each other again after I leave. I am afraid that we will never have the opportunity to share a life together. I have this awful feeling that I won't be able to live up to my end of the bargain and you are going to be hurt because of it," he said.

"Shhh, Peter. Yes, we have minor obstacles," I said, as I moved closer to him. "But they're nothing that we can't overcome. Tomorrow we will pull out our calendars and day-timers and map it all out. Plan?"

"Plan," he agreed.

I knew he wasn't any more relaxed about things than when we started the conversation, but at least he got to verbalize some of it. He had the chance to tell me what he was concerned about. He needed to hear my reassurances again.

We finished packing the remaining items. I got him talking about the significance of this one or that one, and he seemed to be a bit more at ease. We were packing up a small portion of his life, and that only put a finality and confirmation to the fact that his life here was coming to an end.

We went to bed that night and as we lay there together, I easily took on the role of caretaker. I held him tightly and verbally reinforced my love and support for him. I spoke of our plans for extended weekends, holidays, and vacation time. He needed to be reassured. He needed to be held. It wasn't the packing I was there for—it was to console and comfort. He was hurting and scared. There were big changes in his life. As we lay there, I felt him relax. He may not have been feeling any better about everything, but at least he was feeling better about us. His head was cradled in my arms, up against my chest. He looked up and just thanked me for being there and knowing what he was thinking. He was quiet after that, and then fell asleep.

As promised, the next morning, after we woke up and showered, we made coffee and confirmed our dates for seeing each other—which weekends I would fly down and his return for the coming holidays. It was all set. On paper, it looked great, and I was determined to make it work. The simplicity of that one activity seemed to make him more relaxed. It was as if one uncertainty for him was laid to rest. When we finished, we returned to some remaining packing and planned out the rest of our day. There were still parties and engagements to attend, where he was the guest of honor.

The Austin corporation provided Peter with a car, so he didn't have to drive his vehicle down. That extended his time here by three days. We spent the entire seventy-two hours together. The night prior to him leaving, we spent time at his parent's house, with family and close friends. We spent the balance of the evening and that night at his house. In the morning, I went to the airport with him and the family.

I had actually said my good-byes earlier at his house. I wanted him to have time with his family alone, so I went out to O'Hare with them, but I left before he said his good-byes to them and went through security. I said good-bye to his family and to him again and walked away. As I walked to the down escalators, to the lower level where the trains were, the tears started streaming down my face. I couldn't control them or stop them. Vanessa called as I boarded the train. She heard it in my voice and just listened as I tried to talk. I couldn't. I hurt so badly and felt so empty. I knew I would see him soon, when our travel schedules were worked out, but it still didn't ease the pain of saying good-bye.

When I arrived home, the phone rang. It was my best friend Michael. He knew this was going to be a rough day and just wanted me to know he was there if I needed him. I thanked him and said that I just wanted to be alone for a while and that I might call him later for a lake walk.

A lake walk was exactly what I needed. I could usually clear my head and sort things out at the lake. It was a brisk fall day. The air was crisp and there was a chill to the breeze. I didn't call Michael. I wanted to be alone. I walked to my favorite place along the banks of the lake. I sat and looked out at the water, with its small waves and white caps. The lake was turbulent and in turmoil, the action of the water mimicking my emotional state at the moment. I was talking to myself and trying to find a calm place with what I was feeling. I was trying not to be melodramatic about it all. I truly hurt inside and felt a genuine loss. I kept telling myself that it was temporary, and I knew that. This initial reaction to him leaving would pass. Once our visitation schedule was enacted, and we had a visit or two under our belts, it would become a part of normal life for us.

I didn't see the four of them walking up behind me, but suddenly, I was surrounded by my friends. Michael, KT, Gwen, and Vanessa all took a seat on either side of me on the wall. I didn't realize that I had been out at the lake as long as I was.

"How did you know where I would be?" I asked. It was a general statement, not directed to anyone in particular.

"I know you. I know where you go when things are messed up in your world," Michael said. "We checked the condo first and Robert told us you took off for a walk. I knew then where to find you."

"How long have you been out here?" Vanessa asked.

"I guess I came out about 1:00," I answered.

"You get it all sorted out?" KT asked, as she put her arm around me.

"Some. It will be better tomorrow," I replied.

"It is always difficult to say good-bye, whether it is temporary like this is, or permanent," Gwen said, as she patted my hand.

"I know it's temporary. I wasn't expecting to feel this distraught over it all. Doesn't that sound like a drama queen? I will be seeing him in a couple of weeks. I just feel so stupid for feeling this way," I said.

"It's not silly, honey. He is important to you. You have the right to feel any way you want," Gwen said with a sweet smile.

"Has he called you yet? You know, to tell you he arrived OK?" Vanessa asked.

Reaching into my pocket, I answered, "I didn't grab my cell. It's on the counter."

"Maybe we should go in and that way you will be there when he calls," Vanessa suggested.

"Yeah, we can go in. You must be freezing—you are always cold. Let's go," I said to the group.

We all got up and started walking back to my condo. I looked at the four of them and felt very fortunate that they were my friends. How nice of them to take time out of their day to come and offer some support and comfort. As we walked, I privately reminded KT of the conversation we had, when she said she had a bad feeling about the whole Austin thing. She said nothing in return, and we walked in silence.

When we reached the condo, there wasn't a voice mail from him on the house or cell phone. I was slightly deflated. But I knew that there were things that he had to do when he first arrived. There would be checking into the hotel, his temporary home until tomorrow when his furniture arrived. They were picking him up at the airport and taking him to his new office, getting him settled there. I would hear from him.

After my four friends left, I settled into getting some things done around the condo. I checked the mail and turned on the computer. I checked e-mail, and there was one from Peter.

Jeffrey,

One of the hardest things about all of this was saying good-bye to you today. I know that it is all temporary. I know that we will be seeing each other soon. It doesn't make it any easier. I will call you tonight when I'm at the hotel. I am feeling pretty crappy, knowing that you are there and I'm somewhere other than with you. I love you and I miss you terribly already!

Peter

I busied myself with meaningless and mindless stuff around the house. I was waiting for his call. I wanted and needed to hear from him. I thought it all out and had it all reconciled in my mind. This was going to be just like the beginning of our relationship, electronic and cellular—for a while, anyway. There was still something unsettling about it all. I couldn't get a handle on it. Even though I had our new relationship arrangements square in my head, I couldn't shake KT's comments from my mind. *"I have a bad feeling about all of this. There is a dark ending to this."* I was hoping that her feelings and insight were wrong.

As promised, he called, and we spent a couple of hours on the phone. We briefly touched on our feelings of loneliness for each other, but didn't elaborate on them. We talked about his new office and his new town house. We made plans for my first visit. I was going to help organize "our" Austin home—as he put it. We were going to pick out paint and do various domestic activities along those lines. It was an uplifting conversation, and I think we both felt better by the time we said good-bye and hung up.

CHAPTER 9

Winter

November and December went pretty well and as planned. We spoke on the phone and computer, and even wrote a letter or two between visits. It was as if he was on an extended business trip and not as if he had moved away. I was kidding myself and was lonely for him, but at least for the short term, it worked. On the nights that I was the loneliest for him, I would put Elton John on the stereo and remember his touches, the smell of his skin, and that heart-warming smile.

He came home for Thanksgiving. We both had family obligations and still managed to get private time in, after I returned from out of town. We used our time wisely when we were together. We were never more than an arm's length from each other.

Christmas worked out a bit differently. We had our time, but he had to return to Austin earlier than originally planned, as the deadline on a special, high-priority project had been moved up. He was originally going to have the whole week between Christmas and New Year's off, but that was cut short. I was out of vacation time and had to work between the two holidays. It was the first time the plan didn't work as designed.

One of the fringe benefits of working for an airline is that we get to fly for free, unlimited. It is, however, tricky and difficult during the holiday season. Flight schedules are reduced and load factors are at full capacity. I had some distance to cover—Chicago to Austin and return.

New Year's became my assigned holiday to travel. It was looking good. I called a friend who worked in reservations and asked her to check for special fares and possible routing for me. I couldn't find anything on my own. She worked diligently, but came up with the same results that I already had. Basically, I could get out of Chicago to a connecting point or an intermediate stop, and from there it looked really nasty. Any and all special fares were nonexistent.

The fares on other carriers were exorbitant, and even though Peter offered to pay for a ticket, I convinced him that I was sure I would be able to make it. I felt I could, as I had never had a problem in the past, holiday or no holiday. It would just take some persistence, patience, and a well-thought-out plan.

I had December thirtieth off, and we were given the thirty-first off as a company holiday. Traveling didn't look good as I neared my departure date. I was going to try on the thirtieth, and if I didn't make it, I would try again on the thirty-first.

On the thirtieth, I made it out of Chicago, got pulled off the plane at an intermediate stop, and continued to try to work my way south. I was stuck. I decided to give up and head back home on the last flight that night.

On the thirty-first, I had a backup plan. If I could at least get to Houston, Peter would drive the three hours and come and get me. It was a workable plan. I just had to get there. Of course, Murphy's Law came into play, and there were delays between Chicago and Houston due to weather. One of the planes mechanicaled, and paying customers came first. All part of the game. I had flown out of Chicago once already and was advised to turn back by the station personnel, because of the weather and boarding numbers. I did not want to be stranded.

I had been in an airport since 6:00 that morning, and there was only one chance left for me. I had become good friends with the gate agent by this time. I heard her call my name, and I approached the podium. Was it really going to happen? My spirits were uplifted, and I had hope, albeit slight.

As I approached, she answered the phone, printing my boarding pass at the same time. She laid the pass on the counter and kept her hand on it. She hung the phone up, my cell rang, and I answered quickly. It was Peter. I told him to hold on and held the phone up so he could hear what I was about to hear.

The agent told me that while she was printing my pass and clearing me for the flight, the phone call was advising her that there was a flight crew being re-routed, and if they made it in time, they were going to be on that flight. She made me promise not to board until she gave me the OK. I promised and thanked her a dozen times.

Peter and I were excited at the prospect that it might actually materialize and I would not only be on a plane, but a plane that was nonstop to Austin. I waited what seemed to be an eternity. I got her wave of OK and started towards the jetway.

I was surrendering my boarding pass when I heard my name being called over the gate loudspeaker. I turned to see three flight attendants standing there. I returned my boarding pass to the agent and thanked her for all of her help. I wished her a Happy New Year and started to walk away. She called me back and told me to run to another gate, as a Houston flight was boarding, about to push off, and from what she could see, there were two seats open.

I took off running, and as I breathlessly approached the gate, the agent hung up the phone and informed me that the flight was already pushing back. She was trying to stop it, after getting a call from the first agent, but it was already pushing. I looked out the window and saw that it was already being disconnected from the push-back. She apologized, and I thanked her for her efforts. I called Peter and explained what happened. He understood, and I told him I would call him from home when I got there. I was disappointed and just wanted out of the airport.

I called him after I threw my packed bag on the bed. We talked for a short time about what I had done all day. We even joked about me being on a flight to nowhere. We disguised our disappointment and tried to put a positive spin on the whole thing. We were invited to a private party in Austin, and he would be going to that. I had received a couple of invites here locally, and I would probably make the rounds to those.

New Year's Eve was chilly and gray, but I still wanted to get outside and walk. I called Michael, forgetting that he was out of town. I ended up at a local coffee house and ran into a couple of friends. They were an entertaining diversion from my sour mood. I did tire of their constant "we" this and "we" that. I am sure it was because my "WE" had just turned into a solitary "ME". I tried hard not to let it get me down, but it was difficult. I wasn't going to wallow in self-pity.

I didn't dwell on it for long, and the invigorating walk along the lake did me good. I spoke with Peter early in the afternoon. He sounded upbeat and cheery. I was in a better frame of mind as well. He told me to make sure that I had my cell phone that evening, as he wanted to be able to talk to me at midnight, if I was still out and about.

By about 9:30, I was getting restless. I hadn't heard from Peter since that afternoon. I figured that he was busy and rushed after work. I wanted out of the condo. I really didn't want to be out and about on the street, but I didn't want to be alone in the condo, either. I dressed, and out the door I went. I walked the two blocks to Broadway and headed south. My cell rang.

"Hello, handsome," I said, answering.

"Hey, mister. What ya doing?" he asked.

"I wanted to get out of the house. Just walking the hood. I miss you terribly. I so want to be there with you," I said.

"I want you to be here with me, too," he agreed.

"Well, I will be there next weekend. I will make it up to you," I said.

"SWEET! I like the sound of that. So, what are you wearing?" he asked provocatively.

Laughing, I replied, "If this is going to be one of those kinds of calls, let me get back to the house first."

"No, it isn't that type of call—just wondering. Just making sure you don't look too good this evening, while you are out without me," he explained.

I played along as I walked. I told him what I had on. We also talked about my plans for the evening and recapped his. The more I talked to him, the less I wanted to be in the city without him. It just wasn't in the cards for us. He asked my location again and I told him. We also discussed the fact that he would be out on the road, and I said to be careful. New Year's is a drinking holiday, and I wanted to make sure he would be careful. He assured me he would. He gave me some news about the family, and I told him they had called me and it looked like I was going up there for dinner on Monday or Tuesday.

"So, where are you now?" he asked—another location check.

"This precise moment, I am at the corner of Roscoe and Broadway," I answered. "I am facing east and looking into one of the storefronts. My right foot is pointing southeast and the left is pointing east…"

"OK, OK, OK! Don't be a smart-ass!" he said with a laugh "It's just that I miss you, and as silly as this sounds, it just kind of makes me feel like I am there with you."

"I'm sorry—just being silly. I wasn't trying to be mean. It's just a little frustrating for both of us, isn't it?" I replied.

"We will have our time. We will celebrate when we are together. Hey! What jacket do you have on?" he asked.

"OK, honey, this clothing fetish thing you've got going on this evening is a bit strange. Do you have both hands on the wheel?" I asked.

"Yep, both hands are on the wheel. Come on, which jacket? The new black leather or the yellow ski jacket? They both look great on you," he said.

"It's the yellow one," I answered.

"Nice. You look good in that jacket," he said.

I was still on Roscoe at Broadway, when I told him I was going to start walking again. I was getting cold just standing there. He then asked me if I remembered that condo construction we passed on a walk one time. I did. He seemed to think it was on Roscoe; I remembered it on a different street. I told him I was going to be walking up Roscoe anyway and would check to see if it was finished and let him know. I thought it was odd that he was interested in that, but I reasoned that was just one more way for him to feel connected to me that evening.

I started up Roscoe and met up with a friend and his date for the evening. I told Peter I would call him back in a couple of minutes. We hung up with him telling me that he had just parked the car and would wait for my call back.

I talked with them for about fifteen minutes, and they invited me to the party they were going to. They gave me the address and encouraged me to attend. I gave them my loose itinerary for the evening and promised that I would try to swing by. We exchanged holiday hugs and kisses, and off they went. I called Peter back.

"Damn, mister, you are looking good," he said when he answered the phone.

"Peter, this clothing fantasy fetish thing is kind of weirding me out, but thanks for the nice mental visual of me. I glad you remember what I look like. I would hate to be replaced by some pseudo urban cowboy at your party tonight," I said in jest.

"Ain't going to happen!" he replied quickly.

"Are you inside at the party yet?" I asked.

"Party hasn't started yet. Watch out for that lady and her rambunctious dog," he said.

"What?" I looked up and spotted a lady coming at me, with her dog straining at the leash. "How did you know, Peter? Where are you?"

"See the white car that is double-parked about a half a block up?" he asked.

"NO FUCKING WAY! But…how else would you know? Peter, is that really you? It has to be you. I can't believe…" I stuttered.

"It's me, baby! Get up here! I told you the party hasn't started yet. How about you and me ring in the New Year?" he invited.

I started walking at a fast pace, almost breaking into a run, until I started to slip and slide on the icy sidewalk and almost lost my balance and wiped out. When I reached the car, the passenger side window was being rolled down and I heard the locks click open. I was still on the phone with him and stood stunned that he was actually sitting there smiling at me.

"I can't believe you are here! How did…? When did you…? OH, MY GOD! I just can't believe it!" I was shouting into the phone.

"Jeff!"

"What?"

"Can we hang up now?" he said, grinning at me.

"Oh, yeah." I flipped my phone closed and hopped into the passenger seat.

All I could do was kiss him and touch him. I exhaled loudly and began to chuckle, and then we both broke out into laughter. I had a dozen questions for him. I just couldn't believe that he was sitting there. I looked at him as he put the car into gear and pulled away. We made our way to my condo and parked in the garage. We grabbed his briefcase and the champagne from the backseat and quickly made our way to the elevator. We just missed the ball dropping in Times Square, but that didn't matter. We had about an hour before it would be midnight here, and we were together.

I rapidly fired off a few questions at him: "Does anyone else know you are in town? How long are you in town for? How did you manage to arrange this? Are you going to be in the doghouse at work with the new bosses for not being there tonight?"

"No one knows but you. Just for tonight until 7:00. I cashed in some mileage. I didn't think I had enough, but I did. I talked with them and they were all right with it," he explained.

"I am just speechless. I am so happy to see you," I said.

"I didn't have time to go home and pack, so I need some lounging clothes. I will be wearing these clothes home tomorrow. We wear the same size underwear, so I figured that I could steal a pair from you," he said.

"You know where the drawstrings and T-shirts are. But why?" I was the one with the devilish grin this time.

"SWEET! All right, then. Let's grab the bottle and go get comfy," he suggested.

I walked past him to the bedroom and started lighting candles. I came out to get the glasses and bottle of champagne, when he stopped me. He selected the music. It was a special song—I knew what it was as soon as it started.

"Do you recognize this?" he asked as he turned to face me.

"I do—I love this song," I confirmed.

"Yeah, me, too. Do you remember it was playing in the background on our first date?" he asked.

"I remember. I always remember how I thought you were so drop-dead handsome sitting across the table from me. Peter, my heart aches because of the distance between us. My soul soars with excitement because of you. My life is enriched and enhanced because you are a wonderful part of my life," I said.

His embrace tightened as he kissed me. His hands gripped me as if this were our last evening together. He held me close as we danced to the Elton John playing in the background. Elton John serenaded us with "Something About the Way You Look Tonight." It was as if Elton John was performing for us privately. We were lost in time, our time, the only time that mattered right then.

We danced to the song twice, and then Peter kissed my forehead and walked towards the bedroom. I followed. It was eleven-something. We made love as the year in which we met became part of our past and the New Year began and held in it our future.

With the holidays behind us, I made my every-two-weeks trips to Austin. I took extended weekends with vacation time and comp time. It was working out well. I traveled two weekends for the month of January, and he traveled up once. Our time together had to be shared. There were visits to his parents' and dinner with friends. I tried to arrange a little dinner party so that Michael and the girls from work could meet him finally, but it just didn't work out.

February wasn't going to be as easy as January. I tried to remain positive, as difficult as it was at times. I did remain committed to our arrangement. We planned and replanned, but nothing seemed to be working. It was his job obligations or mine—appointments and meetings that just couldn't be changed. We got a break when a required class for me was cancelled. We capitalized on this fortunate event and started planning. It would be me flying, since we had such short notice and fares for him would be just astronomical. That trip to Austin was a success.

The next trip was my scheduled weekend trip. I was pretty excited that we would be spending two back-to-back weekends together. I started to feel under the weather about three days prior to me leaving. It was my annual battle with bronchitis. I was livid. I was proactive and called my doctor, and was given the meds I always was given, which usually kick it out quickly. I wanted to fly to Austin and keep our planned visit.

I normally would have worked and let it play out. It was annoying, but I could function and wasn't contagious. I decided to take a couple of days off and nurse myself back to health so I would be in good shape to travel.

Peter called three or four times a day to check on me. Try as I might, I couldn't convince him that I was well enough to travel. I finally conceded and gave up trying. When it was his weekend to travel, he began to feel and sound like I had the week before. I was better and he was getting sick. He said it was only a cold, but it turned into bronchitis. He was worse than I was in a matter of a day or two. Our weekends together passed and we spent them apart.

When we spoke, I could tell he was worn down and exhausted. He would become winded and have coughing fits. I asked if he had seen a doctor yet. He had and was going back at the end of the week. He had a business trip coming up over the weekend, some trade show that was mandatory for him to attend. I expressed my concern about him traveling, and he was stubborn.

In the past with trade shows, I usually didn't hear from him much. There was setup, attending exhibits, and the all-important and time-consuming networking. Breakfast meetings, dinner engagements, and other activities occupied his time. Potential clients everywhere needed his attention and time, nonstop.

I continued to be concerned over his health. He didn't sound any better, although he proclaimed to be. He did slip and tell me that his whole body hurt—not ached, but hurt. His doctor's appointment was the morning he was scheduled to leave for the trade show.

I had this uneasy feeling that I couldn't shake. I tried to convince him to get a replacement, but he wasn't budging and I dropped it.

I understood the importance of him going. His company was to debut a new product, and it was his department that was responsible for it. He had to be there. He had helped develop it, and it was part of his obligation and dedication to see the project through to its debut.

I had plans of my own for the weekend. I was invited to spend the weekend sailing on a chartered yacht. My longtime friends Samuel and Andrew were celebrating their twenty-five-year commitment. The celebrating couple would be hosting six guests. They chartered a ninety-two foot motor yacht that had one master stateroom, three berths that slept two guests each, all the amenities of home, and a crew of three. The open foredeck was spacious and comfortably accommodated everyone that would be on board. A smaller aft deck was open and equally as accommodating. There was plenty of room for the entire entourage to assemble or leisurely wander about.

This excursion was something that Sam wanted to do for Andrew and had been planning for a year. I felt very privileged that I was included among the special and cherished group of friends invited. When I first talked with Samuel about it all, he originally entertained the idea of taking Andrew on one of those twenty-one-day Mediterranean cruises. He decided against it, knowing that Andrew would rather spend their special anniversary in a more intimate setting.

We were all flying into Ft. Lauderdale, arriving approximately at the same time, and would be shuttled to the marina. Samuel and Andrew were arriving a day or two ahead, spending that time in a private celebration. The charter and we guests were a surprise for him. We would be sailing to Key West and returning to Ft. Lauderdale. The celebration would be a two-night, three-day affair. Our voyage would take us out into the Atlantic along the southern tip of the Florida peninsula and along the Keys to Key West.

The six of us managed to find one another with the help of the limo driver, who met each arrival and gathered us together. We were all familiar with one another—most of us had known one another for a long time. I was the last planned arrival, and once we had our luggage loaded into the car, we were off. Our limo driver explained that we were all to meet at the marina's bistro. He gave me an envelope that gave the six of us some special instructions and hints, to keep Andrew clueless about the three-day outing.

When we arrived at the marina's bistro, our hosts were seated at a small table along the windows and Andrew's back was to the entrance. Samuel had arranged for us to be seated at the table behind Andrew, which would accommodate the eight of us. We were to file in as quietly as we could. Once we were seated, we were to start a conversation. If our voices didn't catch Andrew's attention, Samuel had given us a couple of conversation topics that would.

It all went as planned, and we were seated undetected by Andrew. It was well orchestrated by the bistro staff. They seated us, and at the same time, Samuel and Andrew's waitress approached their table as a distraction and engaged them in a conversation. We spent the next few minutes in idle chitchat that didn't produce the desired reaction from Andrew.

Plan B: I looked at Samuel, and we exchanged bewildered looks. He and Andrew were engaged in a conversation of their own. I gave Samuel the thumbs-up sign, leaned over the table, and whispered to Julie, who was seated closest to Andrew, to stand up as if she was going to the ladies room, and push her chair into Andrew's, hoping that would create a reason for them to interact.

As their chairs collided, Julie asked, "Did you guys see where the restrooms were?"

"They are over there, Julie," Andrew said, pointing in the general direction and not turning to face us.

Julie froze, and a few seconds later Andrew stood and faced us. He was all grins. After our thunderous greeting subsided and we were all seated at one table, Andrew confessed that he had seen us enter the bistro. He didn't let on, not wanting to ruin the surprise factor for Samuel, and enjoying watching us struggle in trying to get his attention. When we questioned him as to how he knew, he pointed at the fairly large mirror that was behind Samuel's original seat. We were all amused. Everything for this surprise ambush had been planned, right down to the scripted table conversation, and we were busted by a mirror, which none of us or Samuel had noticed.

Andrew still didn't have any idea what was in store for him. He was under the impression that we were all staying at a hotel downtown, that we were the surprise that Samuel was being so mysterious about. We walked out into the sunshine, and Samuel arranged for the captain of the vessel to approach Andrew and deliver a sealed envelope. We all stood there watching as Andrew opened it. It contained his personal invitation from Samuel and detailed their celebration plans. Andrew's face went from confusion to disbelief, and once the initial shock wore off, it turned into jubilant excitement.

We boarded, and were given a tour of the boat and introduced to the crew of six. The crew would accompany us for the three-day stay. They were a professional and well-seasoned team. We were shown our berths; where on our beds Samuel had placed our welcome cards and itineraries. He added some very nice personal touches, to make us all feel welcome and to express his appreciation for us being there and sharing in this special event with them.

I took the opportunity, while we were still moored at the dock, to call Peter. I got his voice mail. Checking the time, I assumed that he was most likely on a plane traveling to his trade show. He was determined to be there and nothing was going to stop him. It did strike me odd that I didn't have a message from him. I gave him a rundown of our itinerary and hung up.

We set off from the marina and maneuvered through the intercoastal waterways. We sailed the open waters of the Atlantic, and the shoreline became a thin band on the horizon. We were heading out into a vast blue abyss. It was a gorgeous day for a nautical adventure, and the whole weekend was forecasted to be equally superb. The yacht was incredible. I had never been on anything like it before. I was so impressed with Samuel's resourcefulness and creativity, to coordinate such a memorable experience.

I walked the upper deck of our seafaring residence, drenched in an abundance of sunshine. The ocean breezes softly tossed my hair and caressed my face. The seas were fairly calm, and there was just a gentle listing of the seaworthy craft as we cut through the water. I took the opportunity to flip open my cell phone and call Peter.

I was eager to speak with him and check on his doctor's visit and condition. I had a weak signal, the icon showing only a couple of bars. My call went directly to voice mail, and I left a message. I then checked to see if there was one left for me, but there wasn't. I already had an uneasy feeling about his well-being, and this pending doom feeling was starting to manifest itself.

I had to reason with myself that he was an intelligent man and he wouldn't take any unnecessary risks. He had a doctor's appointment that morning, his second one in a week, and I had to be content in knowing that whatever needed to be done would be. He just sounded awful and he hadn't improved since his first doctor's visit. I thought about calling his parents or his sister Gabby, but dismissed that idea. I didn't want to create any undue concern. I also reasoned that if something was terribly wrong, he would have called them and they would have called me.

I flipped the phone closed, still feeling that unsettling sensation in my gut. I needed to bury that anxiety, relax, and enjoy the festivities of the next couple of days. I wasn't going to allow my growing gloom and doom feelings to damper the joyous occasion I was there to celebrate. It wasn't in my nature to be a drama queen and I wasn't about to start being one at this point in my life. OK, maybe a little in this situation.

Our host had an informal itinerary all worked out. There was a cocktail gathering on one of the two open-air decks. Assembling here would allow us to catch up with them and the other guests. The guest list was comprised of those people who were most important and closest to the celebrating couple. Dinner would be directly afterwards. The dining room was the epitome of casual elegance, with ample room for all of us. With each discovery I made about the boat, I became increasing impressed with how well the space was utilized and the event was planned.

I excused myself from the group after dinner and went up topside to try again to get a signal and call Peter. I wasn't getting any bars now, and my phone continued to search for a signal. I was unaware that Samuel had followed me up. He approached me in stealth and found me in a solemn disposition.

"What has you troubled?" he asked.

"Is it that obvious?" I responded.

"Not really, but I know you all too well. Want to tell me, or would I be prying?" he asked.

I reluctantly filled him in, not wanting to put a damper on the special occasion he had so selflessly planned. I gave him the short version. He understood and expressed concern. We agreed we would try to call when we reached Key West in the morning, and returned to the party below.

In the morning, we tried to call from the cell phone and then went ashore. I found a pay phone and called from there. I got Peter's voice mail and left a number where he could leave a message at the harbor master's office.

We spent the morning at our leisure, and we were asked to return to the yacht by 1:00 that afternoon. When we returned, an extra person had joined the group. It was the minister who was going to preside over the commitment ceremony that afternoon. We all changed into our ceremony attire and walked to the beach.

The ceremony was a charming exchange of their admiration, devotion, love, and respect renewed. As Samuel and Andrew recited their vows, a small crowd assembled around us. When the vows were finished and they embraced, we and the crowd erupted in applause and cheers. We lingered at the beach for a short time and then walked back to the boat.

A dinner celebration was arranged at the marina, on the yacht. The group indulged in a gourmet meal, adult beverages, and soaring spirits. The music blasted as we danced at our private reception. Hearty toasts for extended years of happiness were made, as we individually and collectively showered the couple with gifts, hugs, and kisses. It was soon time for the overnight voyage back.

As we were freed from our mooring and slowly navigated the channel out into the open water, we all stood on the upper deck and watched as the lights of Key West faded in the distance. The reception continued as we slowly ventured back to Ft. Lauderdale. The voyage would take all night, as it had on the way there. It was only one hundred and sixty nautical miles between Ft. Lauderdale and Key West, but Samuel instructed the charter to make the passage last overnight in both directions. He wanted to enhance the romantic element of the occasion for Andrew and him and the enjoyment of their guests.

I was up on the foredeck watching the sunrise, as it flirted with the eastern horizon. One by one, I was joined by my seven shipmates. We were enjoying coffee and lighthearted conversation as we neared Ft. Lauderdale and our time together was coming to an end. It was a relaxed affair. We talked about future plans and made promises to reunite more often.

I checked my cell phone, and it was no surprise that it was completely dead, as I had left it on all day and night in the hopes that I might get a signal and there would be some message from Peter. Seeing no need to charge it up at this point, as I would soon be on a plane and on my way home, I powered it down and pocketed it.

Getting home that day was no day at the beach. I was bumped off a couple of flights, I couldn't find my power cord for my cell phone, and I couldn't relax about the nagging feelings I had about Peter. I attributed those feelings to my lack of communication with him over the weekend. I was sure I would feel better once I was at home and had the opportunity to talk with him. His trade show would be ending early, and he would have no more demands on his time. His flight home wasn't until Monday morning, as he couldn't find a flight to accommodate his time frame. I would hear from him once he was at his hotel that evening.

I walked into the condo, dropped my bags in the bedroom, plugged my cell into the charger, and checked phone messages. Among the messages from friends was a message from Gabby and one from his mother. It was late, so I couldn't call them. I would call them in the morning. Their messages didn't sound urgent, and yet I was skeptical.

I did try Peter's cell and left a message. I was becoming more frustrated every time I got his voice mail.

CHAPTER 10

Stop the World and Let Me Step Off For a Minute

Monday morning, I called Peter's mother and Gabby—no answer from either. *"DAMN IT!"* I left messages for both, explaining that I arrived home late and asking them to call me at the office. The feeling of pending doom was escalating within me. I needed to remain calm and get ready for work.

I was on the train when my cell rang. It was him, and my heart was pounding as I answered the phone. I could barely hear him and make out what he was saying, between the reception and the weakness in his voice. As luck would have it, the train entered the subway about the time that he called and I lost the call completely. My frustration had reached a rolling boil by this point. When I reached my transfer station and emerged from underground, I tried to call him back. Voice mail again??? My brain screamed, *"WHAT'S UP WITH THAT?"*

He left a voice mail for me. He asked me to call his mother and talk with her. He didn't give much detail, other than he was in the hospital and she would fill me in. I hate cell phones! My frustration had now boiled over. I threw my cell into my briefcase. I was playing phone tag with everyone and it was getting me nowhere. I would make the calls necessary from my desk at work when I got there.

When I reached my office, I was a bit unnerved and shaken. I was met at the front reception area by the girls. They appeared to be a bit anxious, and I thought, *"WHAT NOW? CAN I AT LEAST GET MY COAT OFF?"* I greeted them as cheerfully as I could, grabbed the stuff in my mailbox, and proceeded down the hall to my office.

They fell into step with me as we walked down the hall and entered my office. They were making small talk the whole way. I was thinking, *"This is unlike them. Something must be up, and I need to be in the loop about it."* I was thinking it was work related. I was wrong—very, VERY wrong.

I decided to hold off telling them what little I knew about Peter being in the hospital. I got my stuff put down and heard the door of my office being closed. KT was the only one standing there. I was confused. They were a force of three in the hallway and now only KT? Something was up. What could it possibly be? I knew I was about to find out.

"What's up? Why the office escort?" I asked.

"Have you talked with your sister this morning?" she asked.

"Nope. Should I have?" I replied.

"Listen, baby, your mother is in the hospital. Your sister called here looking for you. There was no answer on your cell phone or your house phone when she called them," she explained.

"I shut the damn thing off on the train—long story for another time—and she probably missed me at home," I said.

"She will be calling back in a minute or two," she continued.

My office phone rang, as if on cue. It was my sister. I recognized the area code but not the number.

"This is Jeff," I answered.

"Hey. DON'T SAY A WORD! Just listen for a minute and don't interrupt me," she said, direct and to the point.

"OK," I answered. I started to pace.

"Mom is in the hospital. She called me last night saying that her heart was racing and that she couldn't calm it down. I rushed over and took her here locally. They stabilized her, for lack of a better term, and then transferred her to St. Mary's. That is where she is now. I am on my way back there. I came home and took a nap, showered, and took her dog to the kennel. I am on my way back there now," she explained.

"OK, but…." I was cut off.

"There wasn't a reason for us to call you. You couldn't have gotten here last night, anyway. Mom didn't want to worry you and she is doing

FINE! They are doing tests this morning and they are ruling out anything cardiac. They just aren't sure what caused it. They are going to release her after the tests today, barring any major discoveries," she reported.

"You comfortable with that?" I asked.

"Yeah. She didn't want to be there last night to begin with. She wanted to come home with me," she said.

"What room is she in?" I asked.

We talked a while longer, and she gave me all the details and the room information again. She was a bit exasperated with me as I continued to question her. She didn't have any of the answers, and I knew that, but I couldn't help asking and I must have asked the same questions several times. I wanted details and wanted things clear in my mind, which wasn't happening, given everything else that was going on.

"I'm calling her now. Are you all right?" I inquired.

"She's expecting your call, and I'm OK. Just a little tired," she answered.

"Well, thanks for covering this. I will call her now," I said.

"All right, and expect a call from your niece," she warned. She then became very caring. "I understand that you are five hours away. I'm sure you are not comfortable with any of this. Try not to worry. I am sure you want to be home, but there is no reason for that at this time. That would only send her into a tailspin at this point. Try to relax about it all. I will call you as soon as I know anything."

"I am not going home to pack—at least not at this moment," I said. "I will wait until I talk with her and then figure out what is going on and what I will do. I will talk with you later. Bye."

We hung up, and I took a deep breath.

Immediately after I hung up with her, my niece called. I talked with her and tried to calm her down. It was difficult, but I managed, though I was basically crawling the walls myself. When I did get her into a state of calm, I promised her I would call her that night from home. I hung up and then called my mother.

My conversation with my mother was short. She sounded worn-out and didn't know anything other than that she wanted to go home. She didn't really know anything different from what my sister had already told me. The tests were ordered and they would be starting in about an hour. She wasn't wavering on me coming home. She didn't think it was necessary.

I also discussed with her the necessity of her staying there until they figured out why she had experienced what she did. While she agreed that it was important to find out what caused what she called "the episode," she was of the opinion that it could all be done on an outpatient basis. True, I couldn't dispute that.

She was sure that she would be released that afternoon. I told her that I loved her, and we hung up. It was difficult to speak with her, as the nurses were coming in and out and she was so tired and sounded so exhausted. She promised to call as soon as they knew anything at all or when she was released.

I looked up across my desk, and KT was sitting there patiently and quietly.

"Well?" she asked.

"Crisis averted, according to her and my sister. They are not sure what caused the heart rate to soar and…well, I essentially know jack shit," I said, my frustration coming through.

"Are they doing tests?" she asked.

I went on to tell her everything that I knew. There wasn't anything I could do from this end-all I could do was worry. I did and I couldn't turn it off. It was my mother, and she was healthier than I was. She was never sick, with the exception of a cold or the flu.

The parental drama was on hold for now, and my coworkers all came in and out to check on me from time to time. KT wasn't convinced that the situation with my mother had me as stressed as I was. I asked her to let it go for the time being and said when I could explain everything, I would.

The office had everything planned. They knew who was going to drive me home, help me pack, and get me back to the airport. They had a plan for every scenario, and everything was on hold until I got the follow-up call from my sister.

The first two hours at work were head spinning. I was concerned about my mother, and hadn't heard from Peter or his mother yet. Work didn't stop, either. There was the occasional employee drama thrown into the mix. KT and Gwen were trying to run interference for me. I had not gotten the opportunity to talk with them about the other stuff going on—they only knew about my mother.

Vanessa was particularly concerned and worried, to the point of being bothersome. She, like KT, knew there was more going on than I was letting on. I was totally out of sorts, and she knew that this matter with my mother would not generate the irritability and mood that I was in. She started to inquire; I stopped her and explained it wasn't a good time. I loved her dearly, but she was hovering and I was becoming claustrophobic.

The phone rang, and each time that it did, I jumped and lunged for it. Things were moving pretty fast that morning, personally and professionally. My emotion level was peaking, with confusion and anxiety being on the highest end of the spectrum. At this point, work was not where I wanted to be. I needed to be split into two halves—one half with my mother and the other in Austin.

I knew something was wrong in Austin, or at the very least, something was out of Peter's control. He would have called me already. The voice mail tag game we were playing was very unusual and out of character for him and us.

I answered the phone quickly. It was Peter's mother. FINALLY! Some sort of contact and information. I listened intently as she explained what was going on with him. I sat there paralyzed as she ran through the details. I had to remind myself to breathe. I sat mute as she elaborated and labored over each element of what had happened since Friday. With every word spoken by her, I was becoming more anxious and worried.

Peter was in the hospital. They admitted him on Friday with what they suspected was pneumonia or the severe strain of flu that was plaguing the country. The hospital was monitoring his condition carefully and was guarded about a prognosis.

He was very sick—stable at this point, but very ill. He was alert and talking when he was awake, but still slept most of the time. That explained the lack of communication between us over the weekend. His breathing was often labored, and he was on oxygen. His entire body ached, and she said he was irritable. Irritability was not something that I had ever seen in him.

She was being brave, and yet I could tell she was scared. She was extremely worried; I could hear it in her voice, which cracked and sounded shaky at times as she spoke. She gave me a complete rundown of everything that she knew at the time. She apologized for not calling earlier, but said she wanted to talk with him and his doctor before calling the family and me. I totally understood. I knew and felt she wasn't holding anything back from me. But I felt as though something was amiss. Did Peter tell her everything? That was the question.

I had the hospital's phone number and his room number, and I called as soon as I hung up with his mother. I actually got to speak with him. He sounded dreadful. He tried to make light of it, but I was unconvinced. Fear was replacing all the other emotions on the spectrum fast.

"WHAT THE HELL IS GOING ON???????" my brain screamed. Within a very short time frame, two of the most precious people in my life

were in the hospital. I was coming unglued on the inside. I remained calm, outwardly at least, while talking with him.

I got up to close my door. KT was in the hall, and our eyes locked. She instantly knew something was wrong. I closed my door quietly and returned to my desk. Peter was struggling with talking and was beginning to sound weaker and short of breath. I wanted to hang up, but he insisted we talk for a short time, even if it was me doing the talking. He just wanted to hear my voice.

My office door opened and KT started to enter. I waved her off. She turned to leave; I snapped my fingers and waved her in. I wrote a short note and handed it to her. She gave me the OK sign and a smile and off she went.

I was running down the weekend events of the trip and told him about the yacht and the ceremony. I slipped and mentioned the phone call from my sister that morning. I wasn't going to tell him. He insisted. I explained everything that I knew, and he was concerned. I convinced him that it was best that he save his energy and strength and I would call him from home that night. We said good-bye and hung up.

KT gathered the other two ladies in her office as I had asked her to in the note. I needed to get this over with. I wasn't sure I was in the best frame of mind to run through everything, but of all the people in my world, they needed to know what was going on. Michael would be next.

I started off with what they knew already and gave them the rundown on my mother. There wasn't anything new to report, and I was waiting for the call from my sister. I then launched into the circumstances surrounding Peter and what I knew on that front. Gwen sat and listened intently, absorbing every word. KT was processing it all and formulating her thoughts, thinking things out logically. And Vanessa—well, as if by osmosis, she instantly became immersed with all the feeling and emotions that were coursing through my nerve endings at that moment.

Our conversation took on many characteristics. We were somber, hysterical (OK, Vanessa was), sad, and the foremost emotion was helplessness. I was conflicted as to what to do and how to do it. I knew what I wanted to do, and I was trying to figure out how to accomplish it all. I needed to go home and see my mother—that was the most important—and then I wanted and needed to go to Austin and see Peter.

Our conversation wound down, and we went to our separate offices. I would keep them in the loop as information came to me. It was all a waiting game right now and I had to be patient.

My sister called again in the afternoon to tell me that they had released my mother. Everything appeared to be good, and there was no immediate health threat. I would call her when I got home and get more details and an explanation. My mother was a strong, independent woman in her early seventies. Up until "the episode," she was in good health and had a great attitude about life. She had only been hospitalized three times in her life, and that was for the birth of her children. Whatever this was, I was sure it wouldn't be something she would dwell on or let get her down.

Work finally ended, and I cut out of there as soon as I could. I called Michael on the way home and gave him the *Reader's Digest* version of what was taking place. I promised him that I would keep him in the loop as well. He offered to come by if I wanted or needed him to. I explained all the phone calls I was going to be making and suggested maybe the next evening.

The train ride home was usually my unwinding time—NOT TODAY! Thought after thought ran through my head. One led to another, and soon there were so many that I thought I was going to explode. Each thought was fighting for processing time. I was on overload.

I got home feeling totally drained. The message light on the phone was blinking. I listened to the messages, all from that morning. I needed to add Gabby to the phone list. I hadn't called her during the day, and I was sure she was probably very worried and concerned about her brother.

I called my mother first, and we discussed and finalized plans for me to come home that coming weekend. She didn't want me to come home and check on her. She didn't think it was necessary. I told her that I was actually coming home for a home-cooked meal and not to check up on her. We both knew differently and were amused. I was going to get all the information and details of "the episode" when I got there.

She sounded tired and drained, and I could tell that she wasn't ready to relive the whole thing again. I decided to call my sister instead and get an update, to lay to rest my anxiety about her, until I could sit down and talk directly face to face with her.

I called Peter's parents, the next on the list, got the answering machine, and left a message. I started dinner and took a quick shower. I methodically went down the list of calls that I had to make and cleared the list. The conversations were limited in length, and I gave the short version of what was going on.

I whittled the list down to one all-important call, the call to Peter. While on the phone, I finished cooking and ate a couple of bites, then put it away and cleaned up the kitchen. I grabbed the phone as it rang. It was Peter's parents. The news wasn't good.

His condition wasn't improving. It wasn't the flu strain, as originally thought. He had been diagnosed with bacterial spinal meningitis. His condition wasn't rapidly declining, but it also wasn't improving or responding to the early treatments. Still, the doctors were cautiously optimistic.

Eighty to ninety percent of patients with this condition recover completely, if it is caught in a timely manner. The concern was that Peter procrastinated on going to the doctor at the onset of his condition and with the follow-up visit. The symptoms mimicked that of flu and other less severe aliments. He was fortunate that during the second visit, something had sparked the idea to have him tested and the correct diagnosis was made.

On the upside of this all, Peter was healthy, strong-willed, and determined. He had all the qualities needed to fight the battle. His parents said that he told them that he would be home by the weekend. He was sure of it. He also insisted that they stay home and not come to Austin. Save their visit for when he was released and going home to recuperate. He would keep them updated and call them when he could.

His parents and I were not comfortable with honoring his request. We talked for a short while longer. They asked about my mother and how she was doing. As we were about to hang up, Gabby arrived and I was able to talk with her. She was lost and hurt just thinking about him alone in Austin. She talked to him briefly that afternoon and thought he was feeling better. She was convinced, as he was that he would be home by the weekend.

There was that statement again. It was totally unsettling to me. I couldn't place a finger on why. I was taken aback every time someone said it: "He'll be home by the weekend." It was just a silly statement, but something inside of me shivered each time it was said. I had that pending doom feeling again.

I sat alone in the dark after the marathon of phone calls. It had been a tough day, and I felt like a caged animal. I got up and started to pace.

"Hey, mister. How are you feeling?" I asked, answering the phone.

"I'm OK. Only have a minute. I sweet-talked one of my favorite nurses into letting me call you. I'm supposed to be resting. I had to hear your voice," he said. He sounded drained and worn-out.

"I'm coming to Austin," I heard myself say.

"No, you need to go home and see your mother. I would love to see you, but you're needed there more," he said.

"You may not have a choice in the matter. I don't want to debate it; all I am saying is that I am going to check flights and head out tomorrow," I said.

"Jeff, you need to go home," he persisted.

"I can fly from Austin to my mother's," I said, stern in my reply.

"Your mother comes first right now. Besides, I'll be home by the weekend," he said.

There was that statement again. A cold, bitter, piercing pain consumed me. My heart ached, and I wanted to be there with him. I needed to hold his hand and comfort him. He was being stubborn. I let it go for the moment and concentrated on my phone time with him.

I wasn't going to waste time debating the issue with him. I didn't want to upset him. He was sounding weaker by the minute. I changed the subject. I heard the nurse come in and say something to him. Their exchange wasn't clear, but when he returned to our conversation he said he needed to hang up. He needed to keep on her good side and follow instructions, if he was going to be able to call and talk with me again. We said our I love yous and hung up.

I paced and cried. I was hurting so badly. It wasn't a feeling of self-pity—it was a feeling of total helplessness. I couldn't do anything for my mother or for him. I paced late into the early morning. My brain was on overdrive, and I was formulating a plan. I would set it into motion when I got in to work the next morning.

I knew that I was no longer able to honor Peter's request that neither his parents nor I come to Austin to be with him. I was also keenly aware that I needed to fly home and be with my mother. That left his parents. They talked with me about their struggle with his request. Not wanting to infringe upon his independence and his privacy, they grudgingly complied with it. His parents were prepared to leave at a moment's notice, if the situation in Austin warranted it. It was a delicate situation for them to be in.

Arriving at work early that morning, I assembled the ladies together and briefed them on what news I had from the home front and Austin. I gave them the rundown on the plan I had formulated, while pacing. I asked each of them to take a piece of it and help make it a reality. They jumped in, and within an hour I had all the crucial information I required. I made a couple of phone calls to begin execution of the plan.

I called his mother and cautiously pitched my proposal. I first apologized for not talking with them before I arranged everything and assured her that I didn't want to traverse any boundaries and hoped that

I wasn't out of line in any way. I explained to her that I arranged tickets for their air travel and booked their flights. A discounted rental car and a complimentary hotel room were waiting for them. This was all prepared, and they could leave as early as the next morning.

I didn't want to insult them, and there were several ways that my well-intentioned plan could have. I explained to her that I appreciated the position they were in, the proverbial rock and a hard place. I didn't want this to come across as if I thought they were not doing anything for their son. I was also treading into a very private area—finances. I was well aware that they could afford it and had the resources, but I just wanted to do this for them. I was also entering in a sensitive area—family versus boyfriend. I didn't want to appear to be overstepping my boundaries with them. I respected their family and the core bond that cemented them together. She had also come to the conclusion that it was time to be there with her son. She thanked me and said she would call Peter's father and call me back.

She called me back in a very short time, with a short and concise statement for me: "He's on his way home to pack."

We talked about where I would meet them and give them all the information. I asked her if I had overstepped any boundaries or offended them in anyway. It wasn't my intention, and I was not making any assumptions or judgments of them. I never questioned their concern and devotion to their son. If they were thinking about going to Austin, I wanted to help in any way I could. She made me feel at ease with my concerns and reviewed some of the information that I had given her. With all that settled and in place, we hung up. I would see them in the morning.

Wednesday morning, we met at the designated spot. His parents were a handsome couple, always full of life and vigor. That didn't seem to be the case that morning, though. They were trying to put up a good front, but their eyes told a different story. When I asked them if there was any news or new developments, they became very serious.

"We received a phone call from the hospital in the middle of the night," his father said.

"It wasn't good news, honey," his mother added.

"What has happened? What did they say?" I asked.

They took turns sharing the information that was given to them on the phone. Peter's condition was deteriorating. They were considering moving him into one of the critical care units, so that he could be observed continuously. The treatments and medications were not producing the desired responses. He was becoming increasingly uncomfortable and did not show any signs of improvement.

I began to get this feeling, as if I was caught in a riptide. I was being violently thrashed about and yanked deep under water, unable to breathe. I was tumbling and spinning around, unable to regain control. I felt disorientated. A voice inside of me implored me to focus. I did. It was only a momentary lapse of concentration.

I listened to the update and ushered them to the gate for their flight. After their flight took off, I called my friend Mary in Houston, where they would be changing planes, and asked that she meet them and escort them to the Austin flight. I received a call later from Mary, and she reported that not only did she meet them; she got them on an earlier flight. We talked for a minute, and I thanked her for all her help and kindness. She wished me the best of luck with both my mother and Peter. Now it was going to be a waiting game for the phone call that evening from his parents,

The pending doom feeling re-emerged whenever I had an idle moment. The only thought that ran through my head was him saying, "I'll be home by the weekend." Something about that statement was extremely disconcerting to me.

The workday ended, and I proceeded home and took a hot shower, in hopes that it would soothe me. I warmed up the leftovers from the other night, took two bites, and was done. I wanted to smoke, something that I hadn't done in over a year. I fought the urge for about an hour and called Michael.

"Michael, what are you doing? Go to the corner and get cigarettes and come over," I blurted when he answered the phone.

"What's the matter? Never mind. I am on my way," he answered, then hung up.

Michael arrived within twenty minutes. He pulled two packs of smokes out of his pockets, nonmenthol and menthol. He wasn't sure why I wanted to smoke, but he was going to make sure that I had a choice. He was sure that whatever was going on, it was probably not good. He opened both packs, found the ashtray and lighter, and assembled them on the coffee table. He made coffee and sat patiently as it brewed and I smoked and paced.

Feeling nauseated from chain-smoking three cigarettes, I didn't light the fourth, and sat instead with my coffee cup gripped between my hands. Without notice, my floodgates opened and I started to disseminate all the details of the past twenty-four hours. I talked, he listened. I paced, he sat. I cried, he consoled.

Peter's parents called about the time I had finished my emotional tirade and was calming down. Michael went into my bedroom and turned on the television, to give me some privacy with Peter's parents.

They told me the information that the doctors gave them and said Peter was a bit annoyed with them for coming down to Austin. His exasperation was short-lived, though, and he admitted that he was grateful that they were there. He had a special bond with his parents, especially with his father. While the bond between his mother and him could not be penetrated, the bond between him and his father was indestructible.

Peter was seriously ill, his mother told me. He tired easily and didn't have much strength. His breathing became labored quickly, and he had to rest between conversations. He was fighting with all the determination he could muster. He was lethargic, but in great spirits.

His mother said that he asked about me and my mother. He was adamant about me going home and checking on my mother, she told me. He also told them that he was worried about me and how I was holding up through all of this. His mother told him that I was planning on coming down, and he was unyielding in his conviction that I go home first and be with my mother. He was optimistic about being released and said we would be able to visit then. She assured him that I was going home and that seemed to make him feel better.

I felt better that his parents were there. I still couldn't shake the edgy feeling that had plagued me for the past couple of days. It never went away—it was nagging and pesky, a continuous source of aggravation. I tried to reason it out as being inundated with things coming at me in all directions, but after thinking things out logically, I knew that it wasn't just being overwhelmed. It wasn't that tangible. It was intuition, and it felt dark and murky.

Michael stayed until he was sufficiently convinced that I was going to be OK. Try as I might to convince him that I was, he didn't leave until he was sure. I told him that it wasn't like I was going over the edge or needed to be on suicide watch. I was just drained and a bit tense.

I must have fallen asleep on him. He wasn't there when I got up from the couch and made my way to bed. I found the note from him in the morning when I got up for work.

Jeffrey,

The coffeepot is ready to go. Just turn it on.

I love you, and call me after you shower and have your first cup.

Love, M.

CHAPTER 11

Grasping for Zen

The day was dreary. Concentration didn't come easy. I finalized my arrangements to fly home and visit my mother. It was going to be a one-day trip only. It was a minor holiday—President's Day. Travel was going to be difficult, nonetheless. Three-day weekend holidays always were. I was flying in, spending one night, and then flying back to Chicago. I didn't want to hover over my mother. I wanted it to be a quick dinner jaunt, like I had done in the past. She assured me that she was in good health, and I assured her that I was starving and wanted a free meal. Although we joked about me coming for a home-cooked meal, we both knew the real reason that I would be there on Friday.

Midday, my office phone rang. It had been quiet most of the morning, so it startled me a bit. It was Peter's mom. She had a solemn tone in her voice.

"Hi, honey. Are you busy?" she asked.

"There is a lull in the action around here right now. I'm all yours," I said, trying to be upbeat and not sound as drained as I was. "How are the three of you doing?"

"We are fine, honey, but Peter isn't doing well. He is not responding to any of the treatments. The doctor just left. They are moving him into ICU.

He was slipping in and out of consciousness last night. He hasn't woken up this morning," she said, her voice trembling.

"I'm on my way. I can be there in four or five hours," I said.

"No, Jeff, don't do that. There is nothing that you can do here. They won't let you in to see him—I already checked on that, figuring that you would want to be here. You need to go visit your mother. We are here to make sure that Peter is comfortable, and everything that can be done is being done. I will call you with any updates," she said. She sounded troubled.

"I just feel the need to be there, close to him, and if for no other reason, I could be there for any new developments or change in his condition," I said, a bit frantic.

"It is best that you go home first. After you return home and we know more, once he starts to recover and is moved out of ICU, you can come down and you will be able to see him," she said.

"That makes sense. You are right," I conceded.

"He asked about you last night. I told him you were doing well and handsome as ever. He just smiled, winked. He told me to tell you that he loved you and said take care of your mother," she said warmly.

I sat numb, listening and not realizing that tears were trickling down my cheek. I also was oblivious to the fact that KT had slipped into my office and shut the door. She stood quietly, being unobtrusive. She handed me a Kleenex and then offered me the entire box.

I didn't push my insistence about going to Austin. What she said made sense to me. I wasn't totally convinced that it was the right thing to do, but there wasn't any reason to debate it, either. The hospital had their rules, and I wasn't family, so it was probably better to wait and visit when I could get in to see him.

PM, my nickname for Peter's Mom, did ask a favor from me. She said that Gabby was falling apart and asked if I could call and check on her. I guaranteed her that I would. We finished up our phone call and hung up. It wasn't the update that I was hoping for, and I was becoming more and more concerned and worried. I was also becoming conflicted. I didn't know which direction I wanted to go first—east to my mother or south to Peter.

Quickly, the voices of reason and impulse began waging a war inside my head. The voice of reason won out. It was logical that I go home and then visit Austin when I could actually visit with him and not just sit in a waiting room, detached and not allowed to see him.

After talking with the ladies, I called Gabby. My workday was nowhere near being done, but I was going to cut out early.

"Hey, Gab. I am leaving work now, being released on good behavior. Want to play hooky with me for the rest of the day?" I asked when she answered her phone.

"I could use it. Where? When?" she responded.

"My house, now," I said.

"See you there," she agreed.

I walked into KT's office and said that I was leaving. She agreed that it might be a good idea.

"I suppose I should get it cleared first," I said.

"Done," she replied.

"Damn, thanks," I said.

"Get out of here," she ordered.

Gabby was there when I arrived, sitting in the lobby. We spent the evening comparing notes. We both started to speculate about her brother's prognosis. When that started, I tried to steer us clear, but it was something that was on our minds and it had to run its course. We didn't dwell on it, but his health and situation was the predominant topic.

We shared a strained evening. It wasn't our usual upbeat and carefree affair. Over dinner, which neither of us ate much of; we talked about future plans and events. The subject of me moving to Austin came up. She asked what my plans for that were. I was honest with her.

I told her that I had decided that I would be moving down there. I was going to tell him, but didn't get the chance, because the last two visits were cancelled due to each of us getting sick. I would tell him the first opportunity I got. I described the surprise visit over New Year's and told her that was the catalyst of my decision. I was so anxious to see him that I spent two days trying to get there, and with him doing what he did, I realized that he was the one. She told me he was convinced that I was, too.

Dinner and our evening ended early, with us taking a walk along the quiet streets of my neighborhood. As we were passing by my church, we decided that we would go in and light candles and say a prayer. When we finished, I escorted her back to her car and asked her to call me if she heard anything.

As I walked home, I replayed her comment about Peter knowing I was the one in my head. Did I overanalyze, as I have a habit of doing, and miss out and mess up? I wanted to be sure I wasn't just caught up in the romance of the moment. I wanted to give it a couple of weeks and see if I felt the same way as I did on New Year's. I was now determined that I would tell him the first chance I got.

The phone was ringing when I entered the condo. I raced for it, but was late. I noticed that the message light was blinking the number two, and it changed to three as I stood there holding the handset. I returned all three calls.

The conversations with KT and Gwen were short—they were just checking in with me to see if there were any updates. When I called Michael back, he decided that he was coming over. He helped me pack for my visit home. It seemed silly to be packing for an overnight trip, but it kept me busy and my mind occupied.

Michael left me late that evening. I was exhausted and just wanted to collapse on the bed. I felt like I hadn't slept in a month. My body ached and my mind was just tired of thinking. I couldn't shut my brain off, as I lay in bed trying to sleep.

Peter was in good hands—those of his parents, the UT medical staff, and his higher power. I had to trust in those who were there. I did—I just wanted to be there to hold his hand and be near him. Sadness rocked me to sleep that night.

I called Gabby before leaving for the airport. She hadn't heard from her parents yet that morning. I was going to call the nurses' station that was assigned to Peter, but knew I wouldn't get any information from them, since I wasn't family. I would just wait.

I got to the airport early, checked in, and called KT. Gwen, Vanessa, and KT met me at my gate, and we sat and chatted for a few minutes. KT remained when the other two returned to the office. KT walked me to the gate; I didn't say much. I was consumed with worry and doubt. Was I making the wrong decision? Was I going in the wrong direction?

"He is in good hands," she said, putting an arm around me.

"I pray so," I replied.

"Go check on Mom. She needs a visit, too," she reminded me.

"That is why I am here and going there," I agreed.

"You're about to implode or explode, aren't you?" she asked.

"Afraid so. At the very least, I think I might go postal," I responded.

"What's the word on Peter? Anything new?" she asked.

"Nonresponsive, coma, whatever they are calling it. It isn't good. Something is not right with it all. I have a very disturbing feeling about… well…EVERYTHING!" I said.

"Pending doom?" she asked.

"Yep, pending doom and that fucked up statement. *He'll be home by the weekend.*" I looked at her.

"Well, we know that isn't going to happen, is it? You are not going to miss him being released." She was blunt, but right.

I changed the subject and asked about the dogs and the kids. She remembered that she didn't tell one of her kids something about one of the dogs and left her cell at her desk. I gave her mine. She was in the middle of her instructions to one of the kids when my flight was being called.

However it happened—KT caught up in the dog drama or me not thinking (which would be my guess and the safe bet)—my cell phone ended up in her pocket. We hugged quickly and I boarded. It wasn't until the safety instructions began that I realized that she was in possession of my cell! A paralyzing panic set in.

There wasn't anything I could do about it now. The door was closed and we were pushing back. DAMN IT! Well, at least I had my day-timer and it had all the numbers I needed in it. NO! I left it on the dining room table. Why would I need to have it on an overnight trip? WHAT A FOOL!

I was becoming unglued from the inside out. I absentmindedly cut myself off from Peter's parents and Gabby. GREAT! *"Relax, think."* I rapidly formulated my plan of action. I would call the nurses' station and leave my mother's number with them for his parents. Then I would call KT and get her to get into my address book and give me the phone numbers I needed. That would work.

I sat back and became totally oblivious to time. We were landing before I knew it. I didn't even remember taking off. I was in some sort of catatonic state.

The overnight trip seemed to end before it even got started. My mother met me at the airport, and we went to lunch. We talked about the "episode," and I had her fill me in from the onset of the arrhythmia and what was being done about it and why it happened.

Her description of the "episode" went something like this: On average, most people have eleven or twelve pints of blood flowing through them. She was down to seven, which caused her to be anemic, leading to the lack of vitality and the arrhythmia. They were unsure where the blood was seeping from, thus the battery of tests that were scheduled. In her words: "They topped me off with four pints, and I feel like a forty-year-old woman again."

When I was satisfied with all the details and had my questions answered, we moved on to other topics. I successfully steered clear from the topic of Peter during lunch. I didn't want to concern her with that; my visit was about her. I wasn't so lucky in my avoidance when we got to her house.

"You should be in Austin, not here," she said, after listening to my account of what was going on.

"He is with his parents and in a good medical facility, and with him being in ICU, I wouldn't be able to see him, anyway," I said seriously, and then joked, "I can just as easily fret from here as at home, and after all, you promised me a home-cooked meal."

"You haven't called and checked on him since you arrived," she remarked. She was very observant.

"I have to make a couple of phone calls first. I don't have my cell phone—long story, but I will call in a few minutes," I said.

We finished our conversation, and she left me to make the necessary calls. I methodically went down the list of calls I needed to make. I obtained and dispersed the essential information. I then called KT.

KT was more upset about having my phone than I was. We worked through my stored numbers. I got all the info I needed from her, and we agreed we would meet when I returned home the next day. It was her weekend to work, and she would be at the airport.

I called Gabby immediately; she had left a voice mail for me. The news from Austin that morning wasn't any better than the day before. His condition wasn't improving and in fact seemed to be worsening. I was becoming more frustrated and anxious; I couldn't shake the intense feeling of pending doom. I needed to remain patient and continue to be hopeful that his condition would improve.

The trip home was good for both my mother and me. All of my fears about the "episode" were laid to rest. My thoughts now could be totally focused on Peter. My plane left on time, and I was back in the city by mid-afternoon. KT was at my gate when the plane pulled in and I came walking off. She handed me my phone, gift wrapped with a bow.

I was in some type of time-suspended limbo. We walked to her car, and she took me to the train. I didn't do much talking, and she understood. I promised to call when I knew anything. There weren't any new messages on my cell—maybe there would be on my home phone. The ride home was a very pensive one. I was having a slow meltdown.

There were no new messages on my house phone, either. I called and left messages with his parents and one for Gabby. I unpacked and repacked. I was going to go to Austin on Sunday morning. I checked the schedules of all the carriers I knew flew there, but none of them had anything that would get me there that night. I couldn't imagine why I had not heard anything from anyone. I was working myself up into frenzy, and that wasn't good. I decided to stretch out on the couch and relax.

The ringing phone jolted me awake. It was dark in the condo and I was a bit disoriented. I answered the phone and searched for my glasses so I could get an idea of what time it was. The voice on the other end of the phone was sweet to my ear, but I was also instantly paranoid.

"Jeffrey, did I wake you?" Peter's mother asked, concerned.

"I must have fallen asleep. What is going on?" I asked, unable to mask the urgency in my voice.

"Honey, I am sorry we didn't call you earlier. It couldn't be helped. Things have been hectic and this is the first opportunity for any of us to call you. I am sorry," she repeated.

Although I was grateful to hear her voice, I had a feeling that I was about to get some very unpleasant news. She seemed to be picking and choosing her words carefully.

"I trust all is good at home with your mother," she continued, not waiting for a response. "We are hoping all is good and your visit went well."

I got the impression she was stalling or trying to formulate how she was going to tell me something. I was about to jump out of my skin. I wanted to know what was going on with Peter, but I answered politely and gave her the abridged version of the visit. Her tone turned to motherly and protective.

"Are you doing all right, honey?" she asked carefully. "You have had a lot thrown at you in the past couple of weeks."

"I am holding it together. It is reassuring to me that things back home are going better and it doesn't appear to be anything to be too concerned about. They are working at finding the root of the problem, and she is not in immediate danger," I reported.

"That is wonderful. I need to tell you something, and again I am sorry that we didn't get to call you sooner." Her tone turned grim. "I hope you will understand."

"That is OK. I am sure you have been busy." I couldn't hold back any longer, I had to ask: "How is Peter doing?"

"We brought him home last night, early this morning, Jeff," she said somberly.

"WOW! That is GREAT. You transferred him to Northwestern. He will be close. When can I see him? I can get dressed and be there in about an hour," I said excitedly.

"No, honey, we didn't transfer him to Northwestern." She began to cry. "Honey, I'm sorry, Peter passed away late yesterday afternoon. We returned home with him early this morning."

I was instantaneously numb. I was paralyzed and yet shaking uncontrollably. I couldn't believe what I was hearing. It was a dream—a nightmare, actually. I would wake up any minute and find that I was just sleeping. The gravity of what she said was sinking in. That fucking statement repeated itself in my mind. *I'll be home by the weekend. He'll be home by the weekend.* It haunted me. I went quiet and began to cry.

"Jeff, honey." Her voice drew my attention.

"Yes, Yes, I am here. Sorry…I am so sorry for you and Jack…" My words trailed off.

I listened as she detailed the sequence of events. My heart ached for them. I stood staring out the window at nothing. Tears streamed down my cheeks and moistened my shirt. The pain I felt for them, a mother and father having to say good-bye to their son. How awful and dreadful that must be.

Peter never woke up from Thursday, and his condition deteriorated and worsened throughout the day and overnight. She continued by telling me that they didn't call me, not wanting to concern me while I was visiting with my mother. Then when he passed away, there were so many things happening and arrangements to make that it wasn't until they were on the plane home that she realized that neither she nor Jack had called me. Then when they arrived home, there was the immediate family, the mortician, and all those arrangements.

Peter's wishes for his final arrangements, stipulated in his will that Bill was the executor of, would be followed to the letter. He didn't want a drawn-out vigil. He allowed for one day of viewing or wake, and then would be cremated. The wake would be held on Sunday afternoon. She gave me the directions and information.

She was concerned that I would be upset with the lack of timeliness of their call. I wasn't in the least. I was more concerned about how they were doing and how Gabby and Dianna were holding up. I knew that Gabby especially was going to be an emotional mess. This is one of the most private times for a family, and I tried to soothe her concerns.

Gabby was next on the phone, and as suspected, she was an emotional wreck. She was in a fog. I really felt awful for her. She was the one who my heart ached for. She not only lost her brother, she lost her best friend as well. I listened while she cried and reminisced a little. She talked for a short time and then said she needed to hang up and be with her mother.

I fully understood. Truth be told, I think at that moment, all I wanted was to be alone.

An hour later, I called Michael, got his answering machine, and left a message for Vanessa as well. I then called the other two ladies. They were difficult phone calls to make. I insisted that I wanted to be alone and said that I would talk with them Sunday. I tried to keep the conversations short and was successful for the most part.

Michael called me back within the hour. He insisted on coming over. I insisted that he didn't. We talked for a short time, and thirty minutes later, he was at my door. He had his own key and let himself in. He moved in stealthily and caught me off guard. He hugged me and handed me a shopping bag. He hugged me again and turned and left. We never said a word to each other. His hug and kiss on the cheek said it all. He was my best friend and knew when to give me my space.

Inside the bag were a thermos, two packs of smokes, and a note:

Jeffrey,

I am so terribly sorry. I am on my cell.

These should get you through the night.

Love, M.

The thermos was Crown and Coke, mixed very strong—Michael's favorite and something I would drink once in a while. Menthol and regular smokes. I love him. I didn't drink as a rule—an occasional glass of wine or champagne for toasting, but I rarely drank just for the sake of having a drink.

I located the ashtray, poured a drink, smoked, and paced. The walls were caving in on me, and I needed to get out and walk. I grabbed a cup to go and a pack of smokes, and out the door I went. I walked the lake and found myself at the place where Peter and I first met.

I stood there gazing out at the lake. It was dark and cold. I relived the moment that Peter and I met. I was smiling and crying at the same time. I continued to think of the moments and time that we shared. I was remembering the first date, and vivid images of him flashed in my mind. I stood, finished my cocktail with a rest in peace toast to Peter, and slowly walked back to my condo. I was freezing now. It was late February and I needed to warm up.

My time in the condo was short-lived, as the walls were collapsing in on me. I was pacing, and the sun was about to rise. Peter and I had shared several sunrises on my deck. I refilled my cup, with coffee this time, and went up to watch the sunrise. As the sun slowly breeched the horizon, I began to weep. When I returned to the condo, Michael was waiting inside for me.

"Sleep any?" he asked.

"Paced, went for a walk, came back and paced some more, and then went up on the deck to watch the sunrise," I reported.

"You need some sleep. Lie down on the couch for a minute. I will stay with you," he said.

I didn't argue. I was drained. Michael folded me into his arms and just rubbed my back. I began to sob. He laid me down on the couch, and I drifted off for a short time.

The phone rang and stirred me awake.

Michael answered the phone and then handed it over to me; it was Vanessa returning my call. This was not going to be an easy conversation. I wanted to break the news as softly as I could. There wasn't any easy way, and I really didn't want to relive it, but it needed to be done.

Vanessa was quiet, not uttering a word, as I unfolded the events and presented the details of the past forty-eight hours. When I finished, she was instantly expressive and her voice was three octaves higher than normal. She went emotionally ballistic. I gave her some latitude to vent her feelings and then started to talk her into a calmer disposition. She was insisting that she come and accompany me to the wake. I held to my conviction that it was something that I wanted to do on my own. I needed to do it on my own. This was a very personal and private moment for me. She ended up conceding and asked that I call her if I needed anything.

Gwen and KT both called. I had a limited attention span, and they recognized that and the conversations were short. It was during my conversation with Gwen that I tried to reason with myself. I should be celebrating Peter's life and not mourning. I should be embracing the memories and acknowledging how blessed I was that he enriched my life. I should be, but I couldn't.

It was true. My life was enriched because of him. Before him, I was cynical and detached from the possibility of love. I was unhappy and angry, in general. He reversed all that in me. He made me believe in love again. I love him dearly for teaching me that lesson again.

I was going to internally combust if I had to talk about Peter and what had happened. I didn't want to talk on the phone anymore. I didn't want to talk period. Michael knew that and suggested that I lie down for a few minutes. He didn't pressure me to say anything or do anything; he was just there for support.

I realized that the time had come to get ready. While I was in the shower, Michael put the final touches to the clothing he put together for me. I appreciated his help and thanked him. He scoffed, jokingly saying that he did his best with the awful selection of vintage clothing he was forced to work a miracle with. He was such a bitch at times...

CHAPTER 12

Bitter & Sweet

It was an appropriate day for my mood and the emotions I was feeling—gray and cloudy. The wind had a blustery bite to it. The threat of winter precipitation was looming in the low, overcast skies. The city was void of any sunshine. It seemed fitting, considering my overall state. I was void of any happiness and on the verge of tears with each step.

I arrived and stood in a far corner of the parking lot. I didn't want to go any further or get any closer. I was paralyzed. Muscles frozen, mind numb, grief consuming me. I had to pull it together; I needed to see today through, not only for me, but most importantly for his family.

I walked slowly to the steps of the funeral home, my legs feeling like lead weights were attached as I climbed. I reached the threshold and reached for the door. The door swung open before I could open it, and I was looking directly into Gabby's eyes. Her eyes were filled with pain and sorrow. Not a word was uttered between us. She reached out and engulfed me into an embrace. She held me so tightly I found it difficult to breathe. She began to sob uncontrollably. I held her and tried to comfort her as best I could.

"I came out here to get a little fresh air. I need to walk. Walk with me around the block," she said, as she wiped her eyes with a tear-stained handkerchief.

We walked arm in arm slowly around the block. She said little, and I didn't interrupt her need to be silent, offering the consoling shoulder and providing her with a venue to express her feelings, if that was what she needed. Along our walk, we encountered some friends of the family and relatives, all who offered their condolences and expression of love for her and her family. Each was accepted graciously and with the utmost sincerity. I kept thinking about how hard this must be for her and her family. I knew the loss and pain I was feeling—I couldn't imagine the magnitude of their grief.

We ended up walking around the block a second time, and when we approached the funeral home again, Gabby said she was ready to go back in. I wasn't so sure I was ready to go in.

We entered the building, and the overwhelming smell of all the floral arrangements immediately assaulted my senses. The smell brought on a rush of nausea, as the reality of what I was there for truly sank in. I felt like a caged animal all of a sudden. I had nowhere to run, no safe place to retreat to. I became tense and my whole body stiffened, as I stood and watched grief-stricken mourners walk from one cluster of people to another, talking about what a shame it was or saying he was so young and commenting on how well his parents were holding up. Funeral home etiquette, I suppose.

I knew that I wouldn't be there long. I have always considered myself a strong person who could handle just about anything and everything that was thrown my way. I was having a very difficult time with this, though. In the past forty-eight hours, I had to reconcile and accept the fact that I was carrying deeper feelings for him than I chose to admit. I knew I felt love for him and I really cared for him—I just didn't realize how deep those feelings went.

I was consumed in my fast-paced thoughts and didn't realize that Jack, Peter's father, had approached. He kissed his daughter softly on the forehead and then directed his attention to me.

"Jeff, we are so glad you are here. Cammy has been looking for you. We need to find her." This was all said as he wrapped his arms around me and gave me a consoling hug.

He continued, "You are part of this family, Jeffrey. You were made part of it the night we met you and saw how happy you made our son. Are you doing all right?"

I nodded.

Gabby grabbed my arm and said she and I were going to find her mother. Jack went off to greet those who were arriving at that moment. We walked arm in arm around the room and stopped to talk with friends and other family members. Gabby spotted her mother and led me over to where she was. Cammy was in the middle of a conversation, and I stood silent. As she spoke with the visitors, she reached over and held my hand.

When her conversation ended, she turned slightly and looked into my eyes. Her eyes were filled with sorrow and grief, and yet they were strong and reassuring. She was such a strong woman, and a total mom. I got the impression that she was taking care of everyone that was there. She was offering her sincere warmth and understanding. She wanted to ease everyone's pain and sense of loss.

I found it hard to find the words to say to her. In my mind, there couldn't be anything worse than a parent losing a child, no matter how old. Her face was drawn, and you could see that this was taking its toll on her. I had no words; I had nothing to offer her that might help ease her pain. I just slowly enfolded her into my arms and whispered how sorry I was.

"He loved you, Jeffrey. He was so confident that you were the one and that you two were going to be together. It was that that made him fight so hard," she said softly.

"It was going to happen. I was going to tell him that on my next visit down. I was going to tell him that I was going to start packing. I didn't get a chance to tell him. I wanted to tell him in person," I said.

"He knew," she interjected.

That is when a tear started to trickle down my cheek. I became increasingly aware that I was slowly heading towards an emotional meltdown. I didn't want that to happen. I pulled it together and reconfirmed to myself that I needed to be strong for his family. I would have my time to mourn in private and actually preferred it be that way.

"Have you gone up to see Peter yet?" That question hit me like a ton of bricks, when Cammy asked it.

"No, I haven't, and I am not sure that I can at this moment," I replied.

"I will go with you, honey," she offered.

I found that she had hooked her arm into mine and we were walking down the center aisle of the room. There were chairs on either side of us filled with mourners. They sat quietly, or speaking very softly, some with rosary beads in their hands saying quiet prayers, some with handkerchiefs blotting at their eyes.

I kept slowly caressing Cammy's hand, which lay resting on my arm, as we drew closer to Peter. I hesitated in my step. She must have noticed, and gave me a reassuring glance and gently laid her other hand on top of mine. When we reached the casket, I avoided looking down. I couldn't look down. If I looked down, it would put the finality to my relationship with Peter. I didn't want that. If I looked down, it would be the end. I wouldn't have him in my life any longer. I couldn't and didn't want to say good-bye.

Cammy released herself from our side-by-side stance and placed her arm around my waist, stepping in behind me, and told me to take as much time as I needed. She held me tight. I slowly gained the courage to look down at the man who meant so much to me and whom I deeply loved. Cammy stepped back and allowed me to stand alone. I first saw his hands folded, lying motionless on his abdomen. I felt a tremble run through my body.

I stood there for what seemed an eternity, before I could glance upward towards that beautiful face that brightened my day every time I saw it. I wanted him to say something to me, smile at me, or at least reach up and hold my hand one last time. Those things would never come again, and I began to cry. I soon realized that I wasn't standing alone any longer. One by one, his family gathered around me, hugging me and crying with me. Gabby rested her head on my shoulder, softly whimpering. Dianna held my hand tightly. Jack and Cammy stood behind me, both with a hand on my shoulder or around my waist.

We stood there in our moment of excruciating pain and allowed the grief to be expressed. I wasn't sobbing uncontrollably, but I couldn't stop the tears from streaming down my face. We stood silent, surrendering to the flood of emotions that consumed us. It was Cammy that broke the silence first.

"He loved you, Jeffrey. You made him happy. In the hospital, he always asked about you," she said soothingly.

"I loved him, too. I so wish I could tell him that one more time," I said through the tears.

"You just did," Gabby whispered.

Dianna suggested to me that we go sit down for a minute. We walked to the private family room. I sat with Dianna and Gabby for a short time. I tried to console them as much as they were trying to console me. They made sure that I knew about the service and luncheon the next day. I assured them that I would be there for the service.

I re-entered the viewing room and spoke with some of the friends and acquaintances I met through Peter. I circulated around the room, making sure that I offered my condolences to the friends and family Peter had introduced me to. I hadn't planned on staying there as long as I was. I said my good-byes to his family and started to leave. I was stopped at the door by his father, who said that he would have someone drive me home, or at least to the train station. I respectfully declined, saying that I needed the walk and that I would see them the next day.

I walked outside. It was dark, and a light snow was falling. I paused at a streetlight to watch the flakes as they drifted slowly down and landed silently on the sidewalk. I was still filled with the mixed emotions of grief, anger, and sadness. There was something new to add to the list of emotions, and that was the void in my heart. An overwhelming sense of emptiness.

I walked aimlessly around the neighborhood for a while, with no specific destination in mind. I wanted to walk and think things through. I needed to process the day. By the time I reached the train station, I knew what I wanted and needed to do. I rode the train south and past my stop. I needed to have a word with the big guy upstairs, or maybe God needed to speak with me.

I entered the arched doorway of the cathedral. There were about two dozen other people scattered about in the pews. Some were kneeling, some sat silently praying, and others were reading from bibles. Mass was not in session, and I took a seat and began my quiet and purposeful dialogue with God.

When I finished at the cathedral, I decided to walk home. The snow was falling heavier now. There was no wind, and the flakes lightly floated down. As I walked along, I had this acute sense of not being alone. A soft wisp of a breeze brushed against my face. I stopped midstep and deeply inhaled a familiar scent. It was a scent that reminded me of Peter. It was the cologne he wore that wafted in the air and flooded my memory.

I stood in the middle of the sidewalk searching for him in all directions. As the aroma of the cologne dissipated away, the sadness of the reality that he wouldn't be rounding the corner sunk in. I adjusted my scarf, one I remember him wearing, and I was instantly seduced by an aroma that was embedded in its fabric. It was that unique fragrance that only he possessed being released from the material. I held the scarf tightly to my nose as I inhaled his essence, and I relived a moment of closeness. I slowly resumed my walk home.

I suddenly felt a sensation of warmth encircle me. It was confusing and yet comforting. I didn't feel as though I was walking alone any longer. I felt as if Peter was right there next to me, walking with me. It was that feeling you get when someone is in the same place as you, but not standing right next to you. You feel his aura, his being. That easy feeling you get— you just know that he is nearby.

Reaching the condo, I put the key in the lock and thought I heard voices from within. I passed it off as hallway noise. I entered and took note that there were lights. I didn't remember leaving any on, but then again, I wasn't exactly thinking straight earlier in the day. Still wasn't.

As the door closed behind me, I noticed a shadow move across the wall. It was only seconds later that Michael timidly appeared. He came over to me and started to apologize and asked me not to be upset. I wasn't sure what he was getting at. I wanted to be alone, but I couldn't be angry with him for being there.

"Don't be angry. It wasn't planned this way…" he began.

"What, Michael? What are you talking about?" I was short and to the point.

"I talked with the girls and they are here," he said.

"They are?" I was instantly irritated and grateful at the same time.

I reassuringly patted Michael's shoulder, and we entered the living room. I made eye contact with each of the girls, and one by one they stood. We gathered in the middle of the room, and gentle words and touches were exchanged. Vanessa was the first to start tearing up, and the other two followed. I was surrounded by four of the most important people in my life, and together we had a moment of mourning. We had such a connection that they knew that I was hurting and lost.

Vanessa was the first to break from the embrace and to speak. The expression on her face conveyed sadness and concern. She was fighting back the stream of tears that was welling up on her eyelids.

"Rough day. You look like you are right on the edge. How are you doing?" she asked.

"One of the roughest I have had in a long time. I will be all right," I offered, less than convincingly.

After hanging my coat, I rejoined them in the living room. Michael came up behind me and held me from behind, while resting his head on my shoulder and whispering to me that he loved me and that they were here for me. I patted his hand.

"I need something to drink," I said.

"What would you like?" KT asked, as she headed to the kitchen.

"I can get it. I am not sure what it is that I want right now. Brain is a little overloaded," I replied.

"Well, there is fresh coffee. Michael brought along something that smells very strong. I could open a bottle of wine if you want. You name it." KT was in "mom" mode and ushered me out of the kitchen.

I looked at Gwen and inquired as to how long they had been waiting. She explained that Michael got ahold of her after he put me on the train and she rallied the girls. They came in and had dinner with Michael and insisted that he bring them over to wait for me at the condo. They wanted and needed to be here when I got home. They needed to know that I was all right. She laid a loving hand of compassion on my arm and smiled sweetly at me.

I went through the events of the afternoon and told them that I went to the cathedral to have a few words with the big guy upstairs. It was bittersweet, but I expressed my gratitude to God for Peter and for what he did for me. I also expressed my anger for him taking Peter away. It was a conversation I needed to have. I tried to tell them about seeing Peter lying there and started to get all choked up. I couldn't continue with what I was saying.

Vanessa was up and by my side as I just stared out the window. She stroked my hair and encouraged me to just let it out. I fought to regain my composure, but it didn't happen. I started to pace, and she backed away and allowed me the room to work through the flood of emotion I was feeling.

"I feel silly. I am stronger than this. I just can't believe the void and emptiness that I am feeling. On the walk home from the cathedral, I swear that I felt Peter's presence. I know it was him. I looked around for him. I just knew he was going to be standing in front of me and I would just bump into him. I guess I was just being delusional," I muttered.

KT shared the same beliefs about the hereafter as I did. We had had some pretty in-depth conversations about the subject. She simply stated, "Could have been Peter—probably was," and we moved on. I considered that she was right and felt some of the dark gloom I was feeling inside being lifted away.

"You look pretty wired right now," KT commented, exchanging my coffee mug for a rocks glass and filling it with Michael's concoction.

I paced a bit more as I further detailed the day's events. There was no denying it—KT was right—I was pretty wired. She always had a knack for being able to read me. I finally dropped into one of the overstuffed chairs and fell silent. I was exhausted, and it was all catching up with me.

The four of them instinctively knew it was time to give me my space, and we exchanged lengthy good-byes at the door. They offered to come with me the next day, but I declined their kindness. They understood and didn't pursue it.

I fell asleep on the couch and at some point moved to the bed. I woke early and had coffee. I looked from the kitchen to the living room, and visions of Peter standing at the window flooded my head. He would always stand at the window, sipping coffee in the morning. The images of him were so real and vivid. I was paralyzed, staring at the lifelike images of him at the window. I didn't move. I didn't want to. If I moved, the visions of him would vanish and would be lost forever.

There was a slight shaking in my hands, and I needed to hold my coffee mug with both hands. I spoke to the image that was in my mind's eye. I so wanted it to be real, to have him there again. I envisioned walking over to the window, taking him in my arms, and standing with him, peering out the window. It is what we did in the morning. It was a special moment shared.

I rounded the corner out of the kitchen, and as suspected, the hologram-like figure was gone. I slowly walked up to the window and wept. Peter and I at the window would never be again.

It was Monday, President's Day. The city was quiet, not the normal hustle and bustle of early morning rush hour. Walking into the funeral home wasn't any easier on the second day. I stood in the foyer among all the friends and family arriving and still found it particularly difficult to join all the other mourners in the adjacent room.

Dianna came up from the side and took my arm, and together we entered the viewing room. There was no conversation between us, just a quiet bond of sorrow. I looked for Gabby and her parents. They were approaching from the front of the room.

"Will you please sit with us this morning, honey?" Peter's mother asked.

"Yes, if that is what you want," I answered.

"You are family, and you will always be a part of this family," Peter's father said sincerely.

I searched their eyes for a hint of what to say and couldn't find any words that would ease the pain I saw. Although they were putting up a good front and being strong for all the guests, you could see the hurt and loss they were experiencing.

Peter's mother held my face with both hands and leaned in and kissed my forehead. She smiled and said that everything would be all right, time would take all the hurt away, and we would be filled only with fond and happy memories. She was such a caregiver; even now she had the capacity to look beyond the personal tragedy and pain. She was an amazing woman.

I watched her walk away, greeting people, consoling and comforting them. Who was doing that for her? I needed to find a way or something to say that would put her at peace with all this. One comes to the inner peace on his own—I knew that, but I just wanted to find a way to help her and Jack.

The service captured Peter's total persona. It was simple and sweet. There was no pretense to any of it. I declined a privately made invitation to speak and deliver a personal eulogy. I was being totally selfish and wanted to keep those memories private. I also didn't want to exploit the relationship we shared. I didn't think I could find the right words to adequately describe and do justice to our relationship.

We gathered at his parent's house after the service, where the celebration of Peter's life continued. I spent some private time with each member of his family and those close friends I knew, with the exception of his parents, as I didn't have the opportunity.

I was beginning to find myself closed in and getting anxious. I needed some fresh air. I walked through the kitchen to the backdoor and out into the yard. I found his mother and father there. I apologized for interrupting and started to turn back into the house. They asked me to join them. As I walked up, his father explained that they were just admiring the giant old oak tree that dominated the backyard. They told me that it was Peter's tree; each of the kids had planted a tree somewhere on the property. I stood underneath its sprawling branches and listened to his parents recall a prank that Peter pulled on Gabby from up in the tree.

I took the opportunity to express again how sorry I was for them.

"I can't seem to find the words to express how deeply sorry I am for the two of you. I keep searching for them, and they elude me. Please know that if there was anything I could do or say to eliminate the pain for you both, I would. You both have opened your home to me and accepted me as part of Peter's life. I can only say thank you for being so kind. I loved him; I was in love with him. Knowing how I feel, I can't begin to imagine how you both are feeling. I am so sorry," I said.

"Our son loved you, Jeffrey. He spoke of you two as a couple. He knew that the two of you would be together. He had a master plan of getting you to Austin. Whenever I spoke with him, he always spoke about you and said that you were coming down or you would be with him when he came back home. You were the one for him, and he was sure of it," his mother said, gently holding my hand.

"He taught me so much. He awakened a spirit in me that lay dormant. I am and will forever be grateful to him for that. Not only did he rejuvenate the lifeless emotions in me, he loved me, and that was one of the most precious gifts he could have ever given me," I said.

"He was waiting patiently for the right time and he was going to persuade you to move in with him, in Austin. He knew you were right in waiting; however, he also knew that you were meant to be together and he wasn't going to let it go. He called it the big push," she said, smiling softly.

His father interjected, "We agreed with him, Jeff. We told him to take his time and be patient and it would work out for you both. He told us that we would fall in love with you, too, and we did. The whole family did. We kept telling him not to screw things up by being pushy," he said with a light laugh.

"It was me who screwed up, I think. He wouldn't have had to push very hard. I pretty much decided that I couldn't and wouldn't allow the distance between us to destroy what would be the most wonderful relationship. I was going to tell him the next time I went down to see him. I wanted to do it in person. I didn't get the opportunity." I fell silent.

"He knew, Jeff," his father said.

"But how? I didn't say anything to anyone," I said.

"I don't know how, but he knew. While I was sitting alone with him and he was still able to speak, he told me that you would be in Austin by summer. He knew you were a permanent member of this family and his life partner. He even joked about you being the next son-in-law. His mother and I agreed and still think of you that way," he explained.

"I was silly for not moving with him. I was being cautious and protective of…"

His mother stopped me. "Not silly, honey. Timing was against the two of you that is all. He even said that. He told me about the two very heartfelt conversations you had. Afterwards, when he thought about it, he knew you were right and being more sensible than he was…"

I interrupted and softly said, "I didn't want to be right. I wanted to be sure it was the right thing for both of us."

"He knew that. He loved you for that. He was just going to bide his time and make sure you didn't get away. Like I said, he had a plan and was excited about it. I have never seen him happier than when he talked about you," she said, as she placed a hand on the side of my face.

"Your son was a Godsend for me," I responded. It was all I could say.

"That is where you are wrong, Jeff. It was you who were the gift to him," she said, then smiled and walked away.

I watched as they both walked back into the house, having been summoned by Dianna. I spent a few minutes leaning against Peter's tree, yearning to hear his voice and feel his touch. I wanted to hold him and tell him about my plans. I could only hope he was listening now.

I went back into the house and searched for Gabby. I hadn't had much time to speak with her. I found her in the middle of a group of people I didn't know. I walked up silently and waited for their conversation to end. She put her arm around my waist, and in midsentence introduced me to the group as Peter's boyfriend. She smiled and squeezed my waist tighter.

When there was a break in the conversation, I told her that I needed to leave. She protested, saying that we hadn't had that much time together and that she would like me to stay for support. She didn't need me there—the house was full of support, as it would be for all of us when the silence came and we found ourselves alone with our thoughts, when we required or desired someone to fill that need. We found a quiet spot in the library to have a short talk.

"Jeff, I have been looking for you and every time I got close, someone wanted my attention. I am sorry. I know they all mean well, but I was getting so closed in and just wanted to talk with you and have a few lighter moments," she said.

"You don't have to be sorry about anything," I said.

"It's been an awful day, hasn't it?" she asked.

"That it has. Perhaps we can get together later in the week or next week for dinner. Just you and me. It will be better that way—not so emotionally charged and raw for the two of us," I suggested.

"I would enjoy that. I so adore you for how happy you made my brother," she said.

"It was he that made me happy—extremely happy, Gabby." I reached out and hugged her. "Now I have to leave. I need some private time, as I am sure you do, too. Call me if you need to talk later tonight... whenever."

I walked past my building and through the tunnel under Lake Shore Drive. I wanted to be out by the lake. It was cold and dark. The street lamps lit up the walking trail. I started walking with no destination in mind. I just needed to walk and be by the water. The lake was mostly frozen over, but that didn't matter. I just wanted to be out there. I strolled along the walking path, encountering joggers, dog walkers, and a bicyclist or two. It wasn't that late in the evening—it just felt like a long day.

I was coming up on the place where Peter and I met. I veered off the trail and walked across the frozen ground. I stood facing the lake, staring out into the darkness. A calm was coming over me. My brain was becoming less cluttered with thoughts of grief and emptiness. Being at the lake always seemed to calm me, and this evening was no different. Being frozen next to the water seemed to work its magic. I wasn't feeling any better about the past forty-eight hours, but I wasn't consumed by the emotional rollercoaster—at least for now.

At home that night, I sat in the dark. I stared out into the blank space and void that surrounded me. I was numb and exhausted mentally. I closed my eyes and drifted aimlessly through my relationship with Peter. I lay stretched out on the bed, arms behind my head, and smiled as visions of the time we shared paraded in front of me. I saw each event vividly, as if I were in a movie theater and our life together was on the big screen.

As each event unfolded before me, I was filled with warmth and overwhelming peace. My serenity came from the realization that Peter saved me. He saved me from myself and opened me back up to a world that I had forgotten existed. He saved me from a world where I closed myself off from love.

I lay there reviewing each moment and smiled. I smiled as hard and brilliantly as I did the day I met him. I felt a tear trickle from the corner of my eye. A tear of joy and happiness, shed for having the opportunity to know him and have my life enriched by knowing him. I know I was better off having known him for the time that I did, than not knowing him at all. I heard myself softly speak one simple but all-inclusive word, which summed up our relationship and the entire time spent together:

SWEET.

I drifted off to sleep wrapped in his warmth, knowing that I was forever changed.

THE END

ABOUT THE AUTHOR

Currently living in Chicago, I grew up in a small, rural farming community in mid-Michigan. Growing up there and with the help of wonderful parents, certain values were instilled. These values are still with me today—the sense of family and friends, sense of community, and the importance of love in one's life. After high school, I was quick to get out on my own. There were college classes, different types of employment, and some location changes. Following a move to Dallas, my employment took on a more permanent focus. I was extremely fortunate to be hired by a (then) small Dallas-based airline. That was 1985, and I am proud to say that I am still employed by them.

Having taken advantage of the company's relocation policy, I resided in all four time zones at some point in my career, until I fell in love with and settled in Chicago. I have resided in Chicago for 12 years in the Lakeview neighborhood. Living in Chicago has afforded me many cultural opportunities to experience numerous diversities and interact with people from every part of the globe. My life is enriched with robust friends and a loving family.